ABDULRAZAK GURNAH is the winner of the Nobel Prize in Literature 2021. He is the author of ten novels: *Memory of Departure*, *Pilgrims Way*, *Dottie*, *Paradise* (shortlisted for the Booker Prize and the Whitbread Award), *Admiring Silence*, *By the Sea* (longlisted for the Booker Prize and shortlisted for the *Los Angeles Times* Book Award), *Desertion* (shortlisted for the Commonwealth Writers' Prize), *The Last Gift*, *Gravel Heart* and *Afterlives* (longlisted for the Walter Scott Prize and shortlisted for the Orwell Prize for Political Fiction). He is Emeritus Professor of English and Postcolonial Literatures at the University of Kent. He lives in Canterbury.

MEMORY OF DEPARTURE

ABDULRAZAK GURNAH

BLOOMSBURY PUBLISHING

LONDON · OXFORD · NEW YORK · NEW DELHI · SYDNEY

BLOOMSBURY PUBLISHING
Bloomsbury Publishing Plc
50 Bedford Square, London, WC1B 3DP, UK
29 Earlsfort Terrace, Dublin 2, Ireland

BLOOMSBURY, BLOOMSBURY PUBLISHING and the Diana logo are
trademarks of Bloomsbury Publishing Plc

First published in Great Britain 1987
This edition published 2021

A catalogue record for this book is available from the British Library

ISBN: PB: 978-1-5266-5348-2; eBook: 978-1-4088-8398-3;
ePDF: 978-1-5266-5417-5

2 4 6 8 10 9 7 5 3 1

Typeset by Newgen KnowledgeWorks Pvt. Ltd., Chennai, India
Printed and bound in Great Britain by CPI Group (UK) Ltd, Croydon CR0 4YY

To find out more about our authors and books visit www.bloomsbury.com
and sign up for our newsletters

For Leila and Sarah, and SVG

1

My mother was in the backyard, starting the fire. Snatches of the prayer she was chanting reached me before I went out. I found her with her head lowered over the brazier, blowing gently to coax the charcoal into flames. The saucepan of water was ready by her feet. When she glanced round, I saw that the fire had darkened her face and brought tears to her eyes. I asked for the bread money, and she frowned as if loath to be disturbed from tending the flames. She reached into the bodice of her dress and pulled out the knotted handkerchief in which she kept her money. The coins she put in my hand were warm from her body, and felt soft and round without edges.

'Don't take forever,' she said, and turned back to the fire without raising her eyes to my face. I left the house without greeting her and was sorry as soon as my back was turned.

She was then in her early thirties but seemed older. Her hair had already turned grey, and the years had ruined her face, etching it with bitterness. Her glance was often reproachful, and small acts of neglect provoked her into resentful stares. Sometimes her face came to life with a smile, but slowly and unwillingly. I felt guilty about her, but I thought she might have smiled to greet me into manhood.

I walked through the dark alley that ran by the side of the house. Heavy dew had settled the dust in the air and glazed the tin roofs of the roadside huts. Although pitted and cratered with pot-holes, the road seemed more even and solid than the mud huts that flanked it. This was Kenge, where the toilers and failures lived, where wizened prostitutes and painted homosexuals traded, where drunks came for cheap *tende*, where anonymous voices howled with pain in the streets at night. An empty bus drove by, growling and lurching on the broken road. It was painted green and white, its headlights weak and yellow in the morning light.

The clearing round the mzambarau tree was empty so early in the day. From the green mosque came the hum of prayer, the faithful clustered in a saving huddle. In the distance a cock crowed. Jagged ends of rock had thrust through the earth in the square, a peril for unwary feet. With the rains, the earth would turn into fields of sprouting grass, but it was now the middle of the dry season.

Kenge was very near the sea. The taste was always in the air. On muggy days, a smear of salt would line the nostrils and the ears. On soft mornings, a sea breeze came to chill the heart at the start of a new day. In years gone by, the slavers had walked these streets. Their toes chilled by the dew, their hearts darkened with malice, they came with columns of prime flesh, herding their prize to the sea.

The Yemeni shopkeeper gave me the loaf of bread without a word. He wiped his hand on his shirt before taking my money, a mendicant's deference. On his face was a servile smile, but under his breath he uttered a muttered curse.

I found my father praying when I got home. He was squatting on the ground in the backyard, his legs folded under him. His eyes were closed and his head was lowered on his chest. His hands, folded into fists, were resting on his knees, the index finger of his right hand pointing at the ground.

I sliced the bread, then went to wake my sisters. They slept in my grandmother's room, the walls of which were always condensed with the smell of armpits and sweat. Her shrunken body lay in folds, arm hanging over the side of the bed. Zakiya lay beside her. She was the elder of my two sisters, and she was already awake. Saida was always harder to rouse. She rolled away as I shook her, turning her back on me and grunting her discontent. I became irritated with her, and in the end held her by her shoulders and rocked her.

'Eh! What are you doing?' snapped my grandmother, roused from her sleep by Saida's whining. 'Be careful. Do you want to kill all of us? Be careful! Don't you ever listen?'

We called her Bi Mkubwa, the Elder Mistress. She looked frail and kindly but was cruel without mercy. I heard her muttering behind me as I turned to leave.

'Don't say anything. Don't bother to greet anybody. Come back in here!' – suddenly shouting – 'You little shit! Who do you think I am? Come back here!'

I stood outside the back door, waiting to give in to her screaming. I heard her wail for my father, her voice rising like someone in pain. He was still squatting in the yard in front of me, praying. My mother glanced at him, but his eyes were shut to the screaming around him. She shook her head at me. *There you go again.* She hurried inside for my books, leaving me alone with my father for a moment. She gave me a slice of bread and a penny for a cup of tea. It was the morning of my fifteenth birthday.

At Koran school, which I had attended from the age of five, I had learnt that boys become accountable to God at the age of fifteen. Girls reach this maturity when they are nine. It is to do with secretions. So God has decreed.

'When you're fifteen,' my father had told me, 'It's between God and you. Every sin you commit, His angels will enter

3

in your book. On the Day of Judgment, the weight of the evil you have done will be measured against the good. If you obey the teachings of God, you will go to Heaven. If you sin, you will burn in Hell. You will burn to your bones, then you will grow whole and burn all over again. And you will go on like this for ever. There is no God but Allah and Muhammad is his prophet. We must pray five times a day, fast during Ramadhan, give *zakat* every year, and go to Makka at least once in a lifetime, if God gives us the means. God has divided Hell into seven depths. The deepest is for the liars and hypocrites, those who pretend to be devout when there is doubt in their hearts.

'Every day you must thank Him that you were not born a kafir or a savage, that you were born of parents who can teach you of His Glory and His Wisdom. You are one of the faithful of God, a creature of God. In a few years you will be fifteen, you will be a man. Learn to obey Him now or you will burn for ever in the fires of Hell.'

On the morning I was fifteen, the same bus took me to school as did every other morning. The same faces were on the bus with me, the usual girls sitting together and apart from us, reared into self-conscious anxiety in the presence of men. I searched among them for the one I favoured. Her hair was spread across her shoulders. She held herself with a stiffness that made nonsense of my desires. The girl next to her looked gentler. They were sitting in front of me and I did not even dare ask their names. I thought of dream nights when the blood flows warm … on the morning I became a man.

On the way back from school, I went into the gloom of the whitewashed mosque. The floors were covered with gaily-dyed matting for the congregation to sit on. I went in among them and opened my account with the Almighty.

Clouds of dust rising and rising, churned up by tramping feet. Trees glare hard-headed at the noon sun. Tortured by the power of the heat, the sea turns and turns and wastes and evaporates, and turns into mist and vapour, coagulating in the chill that follows the sun.

As I approached the waterfront I could smell the fish-market. Some of the fishermen were still about. Most of them worked at night, and went home to sleep at the sound of the midday call to prayer. Every night they pushed their tiny boats into the water and disappeared. Some of them did not return for several days, and then came back with a shark or a swordfish that they had defeated in battle. When I was younger, I used to think it was a glamorous and free life, a man's life.

The salt wind from the sea washed over me. The smell of the docks, round the curve of the breakwater, mingled with the rumble of hooves. They were loading cattle for the islands. Livestock did not do well on the islands because of tsetse fly. So, every month local traders loaded diseased old borans into dhows and took them across.

I saw old man Bakari walking along the muddy beach towards the steps. When I was small, Bakari used to tell me about the sea and fishermen. He was always kind to me. Sometimes he gave me a piece of roast cassava or some fish to take home. He said the sea frightened him. He said people did not really know what the sea was like. *A monster*, he said. *Deep, deep, so deep that you can't believe it. There are mountains and plains, and many human remains. And sharks that feed. One day … And the shrill cries of the water-birds. A death pit.* His body was like a wounded, deformed muscle. He squinted at me for a moment, and then he grinned.

'How are you?' he asked. 'And your father and your mother?'

'*Ahlan mzee* Bakari, they're well.'

'And school? Are you doing well? You will be a doctor one day,' he grinned.

'All is well.'

He nodded his approval.

'*Alhamdulillah.* Say *Alhamdulillah* for these kindnesses that God shows us,' he said, and waited for me to thank God too. 'Oh well, I must be going to my bed. Give my regards to your parents.' He waved his arm and walked away, an old man, bent and bowed.

Sometimes Bakari went mad. He beat his wife and children. Once he set his wife on fire. He broke a chair over one of his daughters and she still suffers from fainting spells and can hardly speak properly. Afterwards he was contrite, locking himself away and praying to God for forgiveness, begging God to kill him, begging his family to pardon him. He was afraid they would have him put in the mad hospital. Nobody came out of there. They beat their prisoners there, to find out whether they were really mad or just hashish smokers looking for a roof.

Bakari used to say that God was the only truth in the world. And if He wished to give him a faulty head, that was His business. We can only do what we think is right, what we think God wants.

The sea air was good for the pain in my chest. The tide was going out and the fishermen's dugouts lay on their sides in the mud, the outriggers festooned with weed. The sun beat on the green and slimy beach, raising a stench. Beyond the breakwater, a Port Police launch sped towards the harbour. A ship was coming in.

I knew I would have to go home, because I belonged to them. If I did not return, they would come to seek me. Then they would beat me and love me and remind me of

God's words. In and out of the rooms and into the yard they would chase me, beating my flesh. *Never listens to anyone. He's ashamed of us, of his name. Look at the liar now. What could we have done to deserve him?*

'He never listens,' my grandmother would say, stoking my father's rage.

'Hasn't he had enough?' my mother would protest, hovering on the edges, anxious for her wounded fledgeling. In the end she would withdraw into her room, looking stern. What's the good of that? It was better by the dirty sea, away from chaos and humiliation.

In the distance the ship drew near, carrying its shipload of Greek sailors and Thai rice.

They often told me how weak I was when I was born. My brother Said was born eighteen months before me. He was named after my grandfather, who was some kind of a crook. On the day Said was born, my father got drunk and was found crumpled in a cinema car-park. My grandmother read prayers over the new arrival, asking that God protect him from the evil of other people's envy.

When I was born I caused my mother a great deal of pain. My grandmother said someone should be called to read the Koran over me, asking God to keep me alive. They washed me with holy water from Zamzam and wrapped me in cloths inscribed with lines from the Book. They persuaded the Lord to let me live. Three years passed before Zakiya came. Neither Said nor I paid much attention. What's the good of a sister? Said beat me often. He was the elder. He said it was to make me tough. Said had many friends, and when he was six he was already fucking boys. He taught me to chase stray cats and beat them with twisted metal cables. We raided walled gardens to steal fruit. We baited beggars and madmen. Said forced me into fights with other boys, to toughen me up. Often in frustration he would shove me aside to finish off a fight that I was losing. When I went home, cut and bleeding, he would get a beating. *Next time you get into trouble I'll kill you, you bastard. Do you hear me?* my father would tell him as he pounded him. After a while, my grandmother would intervene. My mother would take me out into the yard. Said would sob his heart out in my grandmother's room. Many nights my father did not sleep at home.

Said was never quiet. He was always arguing, bullying and getting a beating. He would laugh while my mother tearfully appealed to his better nature. He always cried when my father beat him, throwing himself around the room and screaming with pain, winking at me when he thought father was not looking. Said was very big. When people saw us together they said that he would disinherit me at my father's death. When Said was given money for sweets, he paid little boys to take their shorts off in a quiet corner. He tried to persuade me to join him. Sometimes he brought a boy to me and said that the boy wanted me to fuck him. He would whisper urgently … I tried to feel as he did, but I was a disappointment to him. I bought sweets with my money, and always gave him half of them.

Once we were all arrested for beating one of the boys in the neighbourhood. Said tied him to a tree and then caned him. The boy's father reported us to the police sergeant who took all of us to the station. I liked the sergeant because he let us go into the station and play with the handcuffs. If he arrested a thief, he allowed us to come into the office to watch him telephone headquarters. When he got us to the station he took out a big book.

'There are names in here,' he said, rapping the book with his knuckles. 'These are evil people. And once your name is in here, then you go to Court. Do you know what they do to children in Court? They send them to prison in a forest.'

He pointed at me and told me to go home. I fled without a moment's hesitation, bringing a smile to the sergeant's face. When Said came home, all he told me was that the sergeant had given them a warning. In the end, all the sergeant did was to inform my father. Said got a beating. I hid under the bed.

One day, rummaging in a dustbin, I found a five-shilling note. I asked Said if I should take it in to the people whose dustbin it was.

'Don't be a fool,' he said. 'You found it.'

'But it's wrong,' I said. 'It doesn't belong to us.'

'Who said?' he asked.

'Father.'

He grunted his contempt.

'But it's like stealing,' I insisted.

'You're so stupid,' he said coldly, hurtfully. He started to walk away. I ran after him, clutching the five-shilling note. We bought two ice-creams each, and *bajia* and *mhatata* and chocolates. We sat in the public gardens, Jubilee Gardens as they then were, under a leafy, shady tree and had a picnic. We bought a plastic football and went back to the gardens to play with some of the other boys there. We walked home with the football under my arm and two bars of chocolate in Said's pocket. Said said that we could hide the ball under some sacks and then *discover* it there a day or two later. When we turned into the backyard there was no one around. Said took the ball from me and ran to the empty sacks.

'What are you doing?' shouted my father, standing at the door.

He walked over to the sacks and took the ball out. They were convinced that we had street-begged for the money, or

9

even worse. I said we had found the money, which annoyed my father. He said I was insulting his intelligence, and did I think he kept his brains in his shithole? Said glared at me, warning me not to say anything, to keep quiet and take a beating. I told them that we had found the money in a dustbin. Said raised his eyebrows heavenwards. A sudden silence fell over all of us. I did not know why what I had said was so shocking.

'So!' my father said, turning to Said. 'You found the money in a dustbin!'

I could see my father beginning to swell, his eyes glaring. Said started to sniffle.

'What dustbin?' my mother asked, stepping between Said and my father. 'What were you doing? You're lucky you haven't caught a disease. What were you after?'

She grabbed Said's collar and started to take him away. My father stepped forward and pushed her aside. Said retreated hastily, and my mother whimpered softly, her eyes filling with tears.

'I'll tell you what he's after in a dustbin,' said my father, walking towards Said. 'He'll look in dustbins for what he can't get at home. And when he doesn't find it there either, he'll look for it in somebody's bed, having his arse fucked. You little bastard!'

I wanted to say that it was I, not Said ... I was too afraid. Said had stopped his snivelling and was watching my father with unwavering concentration, poised for flight. My mother was now openly sobbing, her body rocking slightly as if she were in prayer.

'I warned you,' my father said, beginning to crouch. 'I warned you. I'll break your neck for this!'

Said turned and ran, and my father felled him with a blow on his right shoulder. It sounded like an axe soaking up meat. Said's knees buckled, and his mouth gaped as he struggled for air. My father stepped forward and stopped within inches of the heaving body of his first-born. He kicked him in the stomach. He kicked him again as he tried to get up. He beat him with his fists, butted him with his head, bit him on the wrist. He beat him until his bowels opened.

'Leave him be!' my mother screamed, throwing herself at my father. 'You'll kill him!'

He knocked her down. He turned on her and snarled like an animal. His arms were shooting out, smashing the air with fury, my mother on the ground. He turned back to Said and screamed and roared at him. He beat him with real anger and hate, the sweat streaming off his arms and down his legs. The cunt. And in the end he stood over him, feet wide apart, and shouted, *Have you had enough?* He stood over his first-born and shouted, *Have you had enough?*

My mother blamed me. I know she did. Said was blubbering and shaking like a little animal. My mother washed him and wept over him. She sang to him and stroked him as she put him to bed. I was the one who found him, that same evening. My mother had left a candle by his bed. When I went in, his shirt was on fire. On the floor beside him, a pile of clothes and newspapers was ablaze. He was lying down, struggling to get up, beating groggily at his chest. I shouted his name and he turned to me, fear leaping in his eyes.

'Put it out! Put it out!' he yelled.

He screamed with all the force in his being. He screamed with a panic-stricken abandon, thrashing at the sheets. He struggled to get up but couldn't. I ran forward, crying and shouting, trying to beat the fire out, but I only burnt my hands.

'O Yallah! Yallah!' he screamed.

I begged him to put the fire out. I stood and watched him burn. His eyes were shut and he fell on the floor and his face was twisted and angry. I ran around him, hopping and calling, stupidly crying. He rolled over. His legs kicked the bed and the frame fell over him. And he burned. His legs were like torches ablaze at the thighs. His face was unfamiliar and white in places. The fire reached the upper part of his thighs. His chest was leaping fire.

My mother was the first to come in. She stopped at the door and her hand went to her mouth. The scream tore through her fingers as if wrenched out of her. She ran in and started to beat the fire with her hands. She beat the fire with whatever came to hand. Someone came running in with a bucket of water. I can't remember. He is dead. I was five. The room filled with people, shouting prayers and wailing. The room was awash with water, and scraps of charred newspaper floated in puddles. My mother was weeping hysterically in somebody's arms. She turned round and pointed at me, screaming hysterically. I didn't hear what she said.

Why did they blame me who had never done him any harm? They all beat him. I was five. He was my friend, he was my brother. He was my only friend and my only brother. Why did they blame me?

A man read over the grave, first the words of the Koran and then instructions on how a dead man should conduct himself in the grave. He instructed Said on the answers he should give when the angel came to question him.

'And when he asks you your name, tell him you were called Said bin Omar, creature of God ... '

For all the wrong Said has done he will suffer long. For all the little arses he fucked, the angels will put red-hot chains through his mouth and out of his arsehole. That is God's punishment.

My father paid for a *khitma* to be held at the local mosque. It seemed like hundreds of people turned up to read the Koran for Said. Prayers were read and eulogies chanted for the dear departed. The *halwa* was served by professional servers, to ensure that the greedy in the congregation did not wipe out the platters before all the guests had had a helping. I had never had a close relative die before. People came to shake my hand, to share in our sorrow. It made me feel very proud of Said.

Said's spirit lived on among us for many months. We were not allowed to sing too loudly or quarrel too often. My father's prayers became longer and his arm heavier. We were not allowed to go to the pictures or attend weddings or dances. My mother hardly spoke to anybody. My grandmother went to Tanga to visit relations. My father beat me often. He filled me with such terror that I was afraid to speak to him. Many more nights now he did not sleep at home.

When he was younger, my father was a trouble-maker. When he came home at night, his walking-stick was covered with blood and hair, and there was never a mark on him. He was a man in those days, a man as men are supposed to be. Some people say he was a dog then, which is not altogether an insult. There is a photograph of him, taken before I was born. He was standing in front of a studio backdrop of palms and beach. His eyes were leaping out of his face, daring the camera with a ferocious arrogance. His walking-stick rested lightly against his right thigh. His left arm leant against a tall flower table. He looked as if he was about to erupt into an uncontrollable rage.

It was my mother who showed me the picture, and I waited silently for her to say something. She put the picture away without saying a word, without looking at me. I wanted to ask about those eyes boiling with rage. Now they are glazed with drink. I wanted to ask her, I always wanted to ask her why he was like that. Why was he so unhappy? Is it true what they say about him? Is it true that he used to kidnap little black children and sell them to the Arabs of Sur? They told me that at school. Is it true that they put him in prison because he ruptured a little boy?

I could not believe that such things were true. Then his rages were so real, so fierce and devastating, that he seemed capable of any cruelty. His lips were fat and lined with cracks that sometimes bled in the dry heat. He looked taller than he really was. His arms were thick and lumpy with muscles. His close-cropped hair was flecked with grey. Said would have grown to be like him, and my father would have looked at him with pride. He hectored me about respect and obedience, when never in my life had I sought to challenge or thwart him. I lived in terror of him. Sometimes I cried as soon as I was in his presence. His cruelties were inflicted with such passion.

Once, when I was ill, my mother spread my bedding on the floor beside her, in case I needed attention during the night. I was proud of my illness, and proud of my exalted position near her. So often she did not let me come near. Oh, she cared for me and fed me and picked lice out of my hair, but she did not let me come near. And I could never forget how she had stood screaming her loss, with her finger pointed at me. But on this night she stroked me and put me to sleep with a strange, sweet liquid which she said was good for me.

When I woke up, my father was leaning against her bed. The door was open, and the hurricane lamp that was left burning in the hallway through the night, lit up part of the room. I could not see him clearly, and I wish I never had. The bed was behind the shadow of the door. He smelt drunk. He tried to hide his drinking from us because he was ashamed of it. I saw him holding my mother's wrist and whispering. It was the first time I had seen him touch her like that. Suddenly he straightened, then leaned forward and hit her. He started whispering again, more loudly this time.

'You're trying to keep me out. Because of him! What good is he anyway? Oh my mother, why do you want to annoy me?'

My mother tried to hush him, and I saw her hand reach out for his face. He brushed her hand away and leaned back.

'Why do you have to bring him here?' he asked in a voice I did not know, appealing to her. 'You're trying to keep me out ... for that dirty little murderer. What do you take me for, you snivelling bitch?'

He struck her again, and again, grunting heavily. And again. He struggled onto the bed and pulled away the kanga she was wearing around her. My mother did not struggle and did not speak. She groaned, it seemed involuntarily, every now and again I shut my eyes tightly and I heard his body moving on top of her. I heard him groaning and muttering, his voice coming thick and muffled off the bed. My grandmother's door opened. My father paused, head raised as if waiting for her approach. Then he chuckled.

'Come and see, my old woman,' he called. 'Come and watch me killing her.'

Then he began again, whispering and muttering, and fucking her. After a while there was silence. I heard him sobbing. I heard him lifting himself up, and through my tears I saw him leaning over me. *Get out*, he said. I struggled on all fours out of the room. My grandmother was standing

15

outside in the hallway. I started to crawl towards her, feeling weak and feeble from the fever. Slowly she turned and went to her room and closed the door behind her. I heard the bolt gently slide home. I spent the night curled up outside my grandmother's door.

I could only feel terror and loathing for the world they had brought me into.

My mother hid from me even more, but I stalked her, waited for her. Fleetingly, when her eyes strayed to mine, I caught a glimpse of her shame, and my heart broke for her. But I could not forget how she had stood with her finger of blame.

I watched the tide recede beyond the breakwater, and listened for the hiss of waves breaking against the stones. Hunger was making my equivocations by the sea more pathetic with every minute. What could be so wrong with the world when God awaited us all with his Hell and his Heaven and his legion of torturers?

I had become a man without knowing what it was like to touch a woman with evil in my heart. Such talk of death when life had not started yet. I was told that God had said that to play with yourself was sinful, that your penis shrinks, and you use up all your *manii* so that later on you can't make children. The doctor had said: *You masturbate a lot, no?* I had gone to see him about the pain in my chest. He was gratified by my look of guilty surprise. He told me that he had studied psychology, and offered to analyse me on the spot.

'It's not good for you,' he said. 'It takes all your strength away. It makes your bones weak. Listen, it sounds hollow. I'll give you some pills. Tell your mother to give you a lot of meat to eat and milk to drink.'

And an ostrich-feather canopy to shield you while you stroll in the heat of the day. I drew blood and wrote with it, drew a treaty with myself. But God made girls pretty and gave their bodies a pungent smell. I had a wash afterwards, from head to toe. None of the other boys bothered washing afterwards. They didn't have a pain in the chest.

I picked up my books and started off for home. The beach behind me was drying out in the sun, raising the stench of ages. In the old days, slaves who had refused conversion had gone to that beach to die. They had floated with the flotsam and dead leaves, weary of the fight, their black skins wrinkled with age, their hearts broken. My poor fathers and grandfathers, my poor mothers and grandmothers, chained to rings in a stone wall.

I walked the familiar lanes and alleys, avoiding the main streets. In a clearing between houses I saw an old man squatting on the ground, scratching the scaly skin of his testicles as he concentrated on forcing out a lump of shit. He turned to look at his efforts, the thread of his amulet digging deep into the flabby muscles of his neck. He grinned when he saw me. He forced out a whistle of angry smell, his brow suffused with sweat in the sun. He stood up, straightening painfully, and walked to the nearest wall to urinate.

By the Welfare Office, I ran up the steps, not daring to breathe the smell of old urine. I crossed the main road, empty in mid-afternoon, and turned into the alley by the Public Baths. There was a powerful smell of clogged drains and mould. Round the corner, an old man was dozing, perched on the cashbox of his fruit and vegetable shop. Rotting fruit, punctured and oozing, lay on the pavement. Wet streaks of sugary mango juice were extended by tyre marks in all directions.

'Here you will only turn into a cabbage.'

So my teacher told me, while I helped him register the winners on School Sports Day. Red card for the winner, blue card for second, green card for third. Why cabbage? He had studied in England, and on his return had rediscovered God and embraced him with unusual intensity. 'What do you want to do with your life? Go away, make something of yourself. What about England? Godless country, but there are opportunities there. What do you want to be? A doctor?'

Was it very cold? I would pass away lonely hours imagining myself a doctor in England. Walking down a long corridor, wearing a white coat and dark horn-rimmed spectacles, looking like Gregory Peck. All my patients are women and invariably need mouth-to-mouth resuscitation.

'What chance have you got if you stay here?' my teacher asked me. 'The best you'll do will be a job in a bank, or become a teacher. Unless you have powerful relatives I don't know about.

'There is no dishonour in becoming a bank clerk. It is all *rizki*, the bounty of God, but it is not what the country needs. We need engineers, doctors, graduates. We don't need philosophers and story-tellers but forestry officers, scientists and veterinary surgeons. Culture is for the rich. Culture is decadence. Look at Rome. Look at Persia. Look at Baghdad, look at Cairo. What did culture bring them but ruin?'

He taught us English literature, and was often moved into long harangues on the destructive ignorance of European arrogance. 'Chemistry, algebra, astronomy … all these were things that Muslims taught to the backward Europeans. But then the Muslims gave up the discipline of the desert. They wanted banquets and festivals and luxury. Their enemies soon destroyed them, because they knew in their barbarian hearts that culture is decadence. So don't worry your head with this Shakespeare. A lot of people say he didn't even exist anyway, or that if he did, he was an eastern sage whose work was translated into English.

18

You know what these Europeans are like. This Jane Austen, I think she's English, don't you? Hoity-toity big red nose and a little mouth.'

But this was in the days when the British were still our masters, and our teacher would clown his anxiety by running to the classroom door and peeping out, in case the Welshman who was our headmaster was walking down the corridor. Then he would come back and continue his harangue. Our poor teacher, he did not know it yet, but his days were numbered. The British were about to go, and the day of vengeance was drawing near.

My mother was married to my father when she was sixteen. Her father was a lorry driver who also owned a shop in a small village near Jinja in Uganda. My father was in his twenties at the time and was known to be a troublemaker. My grandmother thought that a woman would cure him of his interest in anuses. The wife of an ivory trader who made frequent trips up-country told my grandmother of this girl who was a beauty comparable to a heroine of the *Alfu Leila u Leila*. The idea of a pretty, simple country girl for a daughter attracted my grandmother. After many repetitions of my mother's praises, and after many significant pauses and arch glances under lowered eyebrows, the two women hatched their scheme.

The idea did not immediately appeal to my father. He did not see any need for it. In the end he made no objection, nor did the girl's father, although he knew that my father was a shiftless hooligan. He was afraid that left to her own for too long, my mother might turn to one of the up-country blacks for a lover.

My mother was never consulted. She found herself betrothed to a good-looking man, and she adored him. She was a timid, ignorant country girl. When she travelled to the coast for her wedding, it was the first time she had ever left home.

My father was unfaithful from the start. She knew of his unfaithfulness. She could smell it on him when he came home for her. At first she had cried and accepted it as the way of the world, and kept her shame to herself. Then he started to beat her because of her hurt silences. My grandmother told her that marriages were like that, but that things would work out in the end.

He beat us too, and then my mother only looked stern, reluctant to challenge him in front of us. She did nothing but medicate our bruises and cuts, and moan and sing comfortingly to us, and stroke us with her gentle care. She did not teach us to hate him. We would have been better armed with hate.

He beat me when I refused to go to the mosque. He said I had turned against my Creator. He picked up a sandal and threw it at me.

'Come on, get out. The *muadhin* has called,' he said.

In the languor of the afternoon, in the gloom of the shade of the mango trees drifted his muted call. I stood outside the door and heard him mourn my waywardness.

'What happens to these children? Fourteen years old and he's tired of God already. He used to pray and attend meetings and study good books. Imam Musa told me he was born to be a scholar. Now look at him!'

Nobody had told Imam Musa, but at twelve I also started some serious masturbating. God punished me for every stroke of my hand. In the end I gave up God and stopped listening to lying old scholars who could emphasise a point with one tensely outstretched forefinger while the other searched for a little boy's anus. I started to play football instead.

I don't know how he knew I was standing there but he came out of the room as if expecting to find me. He stared at me for a moment, his face hardening with anger. I did not say anything. I had dried up: a wasted wadi, a grazing bison, a sitting duck for the thick-armed hunter.

'Get out!' he said, his voice deep and level, but his face vicious with anger. 'Go to the mosque. Get going, *khanith wahid*!'

That was in the last months while my sins were his, before I became a man. I began to regret that I had not gone. I could feel tears forming in my eyes. They always did, at every confrontation.

'Now!' he shouted, moving towards me.

He came very near me, his eyes bulging out of his face, sweat glistening on his brow. His mouth was open. *He'll kill me*, I thought.

'What did you say?' he shouted as if his lungs were bursting inside him.

'I said no,' I repeated.

He looked surprised. He looked lost. From me and from Said. He shook his head. For me and for Said, and for all the beatings and the humiliations and the terror of all those years.

'I swear I'll break every bone in your body if you don't go. *Wallahi* I'll kill you,' he said calming himself down and looking up briefly as he swore in the sight of God. 'Go now.'

'I don't want to go,' I said, moving slowly away from him.

'May God forgive you,' he said. 'When you meet your Master on the Day of Judgment ...'

'I have no Master,' I said.

'In God's name ...' he said, looking frightened.

'There is no God,' I said, getting cocky.

21

He smiled and stared at me without speaking. He bolted the front door and then walked over towards me. I stood quite still. He slapped me on the face again and again, asking me if there was no God. I tried not to cry. I tried not to run. He was getting angrier with every blow. I cursed him and abused him silently, but then the pain became more than I could bear and I started to cry. He lost all restraint and hit me wherever he could reach. I screamed and yelled, louder and louder. *Lord forgive me, Lord God that is the only God, God of all creatures. Make me see, make me see. God that has no father and no son, oh God my Master pity me that does not deserve your pity …*

'God is Great!' screamed my father in his joy, kicking me in the ribs.

My grandmother told me that she had always felt a premonition in her breasts, that I would feed and grow on the love of the family, and one day turn against it. She wriggled with anticipation and righteous pleasure as she told me of the torments that awaited me in this life. She told me of diseases that afflicted the eyes, the bowels and the genitals of heretics. *What will you worship now?* she asked me.

My mother told me to beg forgiveness, that I should not read so many books. She said that if I lost God I would be on my own in a world that was full of danger. She told me to look for God, to try again, to ask forgiveness.

The worst pangs of hunger had left me as I walked the streets, and I turned away from the road home and headed for the creek. I walked over the bridge across the little stream that ran into the creek and turned to watch the water sink into the sea. In the distance was the thin dark line of the wireless tower. The sea stretched endlessly, without the breakwater to interrupt my vision. I watched the shimmering delight of the waves as they came in, felt their strength and the depth from which they came.

A man walked past me and then stopped and turned and stared at me. I groaned to myself. He came back and stood next to me, leaning on the bridge and staring out to sea in that empty afternoon. I could sense his bulk beside me. I knew he was after my arse. I glanced quickly at him, and he caught my eye and leered. I heaved off the parapet. He straightened too, smiling and looking dangerous. I tried not to look nervous. *Nice view*, he said, smiling at his little victory. He spoke with just a hint of teasing, with just a hint of love-talk. He turned again towards the sea.

'Very pretty,' he said. He turned a full, fleshy grin on me. His teeth were flecked with bits of food and tobacco stains. His chin was covered with tiny pimples that spread from under his lip to the heavy folds of skin above his Adam's apple. His lips were thick and covered with loose, dead skin. Bits of wool and mud and grass had matted into his hair. His thick neck bulged out of a shirt that was stained green under the armpits. He was my nightmare of a sadistic bugger, a rapist.

'Beautiful,' he said, allowing the word to pass his lips slowly while his eyes wandered over me. His tongue stroked his lips in a parody of sensuality. He waited, smiling at me. With a sudden grimace, he cleared his throat and spat a lump of yellow phlegm into the water. He swallowed rapidly to moisten his dry throat. He turned back to me and there was a hard calculating look in his eyes. I looked for a long moment at his repulsive face, and I saw him smile contentedly to himself, biding his time.

'How old are you?' he asked after a while.

'Haven't I seen you with my father?' I asked him.

'I haven't done anything,' he said. 'What are you trying to say?'

I smiled at his terror and started to walk away.

'If you need any money don't be afraid to ask,' he shouted after me. I heard him laugh and it required an effort to prevent myself from breaking into a run.

I was tired of fighting off bashas. In my first year at school, Abbas, a classmate, had given me a penny every day of the school year to soften me up for the big fuck. On a day he was to go for a dental check-up, he came into school especially to give me my penny. His family was rich and he commanded the services of all the thugs in the class. I was to be seen as his plaything, on his payroll. Sometimes he stared at me all morning, through English, Arithmetic and Nature Study, knowing that the teacher and the other children were watching him with knowing smirks. If I looked in his direction, he would slowly wet his lips with his tongue. I knew that one day he would try to touch me, he would try to shame me in front of all the other boys. I thought that if he did I would bring a knife to school and kill him.

I was grateful for his money. By the time we came to the seduction scene he was paying me a shilling a day, and we were both much older. We laughed away the moment we had both been dreading for years.

It was assumed that if you were quiet and frail then you could be forced into a corner and fucked. In my first years at school I fought often to dissuade aspiring lovers. It was not necessary to win these fights and I almost never did. What was important was to show that you would fight however unequal the battle. To many of the boys it was just a sport, a way of showing off their masculinity and virility. The teachers smiled at it too. I could have done with Said.

I felt that God had put a blemish on me, that He was punishing me for Said's excesses. I thought that the torment would never end. I never spoke of it to anybody at home. I was too ashamed. I felt that if I was treated this way, there was something in me that made the boys do it. Then I won a fight.

Walking home after school one day, I met Sud, one of my tormenters. He followed me, telling me how much he loved me and how much he was willing to pay for me. It was three shillings, I think. I stopped to wait for him. He blew me long slobbering kisses as he approached. He came up to me and caressed my cheek with his hand and then slowly kissed his fingers one by one. The loafers sitting outside the tea-house across the road from us cheered him for every kiss. Sud turned with a smile to acknowledge them. I leapt on him then, smashing my fist into his face, and falling on him with my knee buried in his crotch. I punched his face with manic fury. My fists hurt me as I hit him and the knuckles of my left hand were bleeding. I did not feel much pain then. His mouth and nose were leaking blood and his eyes were filled with fear. He struggled from under me and ran.

I stopped only long enough to raise a fist at the tea-house bums before running after him. I could see Sud's friends rushing to the rescue. I hurled Sud to the ground, landing a few more joyful blows before his friends arrived. He struggled from me and crawled under a vegetable stall. I waited until his friends reached us, daring them to avenge their craven friend.

After that the teasing seemed to stop. I was even approached by boys who wanted to be fucked. After a while you began to weigh every kindness, to doubt every stranger you met. At times you ran screaming from a well-meant compliment or you misunderstood a helping hand. That was how you protected yourself.

Next door to us was a brothel. Two men and two women lived in the house with the old man brothel-keeper. All four seemed dirty and frightening, and invariably drunk. They were the whores that men paid to sate their lusts on. I found it hard to believe that anybody could get any pleasure out of those tired broken bodies.

Then that man on the bridge ... big and shameless, with a face and a body that time had depraved. I could see Said in him, Said as he would have become.

After the funeral, my father said: *God will make you pay for the boy's death*. My grandmother said I had stood and watched him die a terrible death. *What hope is there*, she said, *when brother murders brother?* My mother told me to stop crying and that I could not help what had happened. They made me live years of guilt for a wrong I had not done. And then it was possible to hone self-hate and remorse into a tool for causing pain. Creatures rose in the night to suck my blood and bloat me with waste and sin. I fought them in the way they had shown me. I paid them back pain for pain, silence for silence. I learnt how to reject them.

There were times when I tried to talk to my mother, to tell her how things were, and to feel her stroking me with her particular gentleness. I wanted to tell her of the fury of the sea as it battered the beach and of the wails I had heard while standing on the bridge. I tried to tell her that I had heard my grandfathers weep, felt the heat that crinkled their brows, felt the retch that built up in their guts, the odour of maize and suffering in their farts.

But I could see the pain that I caused her, and thought that she could not bring herself to forget her loss. I made her say to me: *Said was our first-born. He was dear to us.*

26

And you watched him die … In my fantasies I made her say that to me. She hushed me with tales of angels hovering in the air, of streams running with honey, of gentle music in the air. She was the same woman I had seen all my life, always in pain, always unable to give comfort or to find comfort, not knowing how.

'You shame me,' she said to me the week before I became a man. 'You know nothing of your father's struggles. He tells me you pass him in the street and you don't even greet him. If you hate him that much why don't you leave? You eat the food we put before you and you don't spare a thought for him. He sits at the docks all day filling in forms for people who can't write. Who do you think he does that for? Can't you at least show him some respect? Don't start crying again, hush! You're almost a man. How did you come to be this way? How have we failed you?'

I cried then, and she held me in her arms and rocked me, and I felt as I had wanted to feel as a child, powerless in the hands of those who knew better. It is strange now to think that we could all live like that, absorbed with our resentments and hates.

The beach bleached by the sun, bone-white sand. Tiny crabs were digging holes to hide from my feet. I pursued one and killed it, and gave it a solemn burial before I set off for home.

2

Manhood arrived largely unremarked: no slaying of a ram, no staff and scroll and the command to go seek God and fortune. There were occasional jokes about finding me a wife. My father made the jokes, my mother scotched them with a fierce look.

The boys at school knew that they were now men. If we could, we refused to obey a teacher who commanded too brusquely. We all began talking seriously about *the future*. Independence was just round the corner, and we spoke of the opportunities that it would bring to us. That was not the way it turned out, and I think we knew that even as we deluded ourselves with visions of unity and racial harmony. With our history of the misuse and oppression of Africans by an alliance of Arabs, Indians and Europeans, it was naïve to expect that things would turn out differently. And even where distinctions were no longer visible to the naked eye, remnants of blood were always reflected in the division of the spoils of privilege. As the years passed, we bore with rising desperation the betrayal of the promise of freedom.

After three years of independence, it was clear that the future had to be sought elsewhere. On the verge of leaving school, I lay in wait for my father one afternoon. I had to wait for him to rise from his nap, wash and get changed. It was late by the time he was ready, looking smart and carrying a subtle scent of prosperity. He stood smiling for a while, repeating the word *England* softly. I thought he would laugh and walk away, throwing an apt proverb over his shoulder.

'Are you thinking of a scholarship?' he asked at last.

I nodded. He smiled and shook his head.

'You won't get it,' he said.

I nodded. He sat down and crossed his legs, leaning back in the chair, chin in hand.

Since independence he had found himself an office job in the Ministry of Works. He had recast himself as a respectable and relatively eminent member of the community. He had not abandoned his old friends entirely, but now saw them discretely and less regularly. He dressed the part now and perfumed himself with sandalwood. He still chased whores, though, and still staggered home drunk on some nights.

We were sitting in the guest-room, which I can never dissociate from Said's death, our legs almost touching. He carefully brushed dust off his cuffs, sighed patiently and raised interrogative eyebrows at me.

'So ... where will you get the money?' he asked. 'This government won't give it to you, be you as clever as the devil. They don't waste their money on *Arabi rangi rangi*. Unless you want to go to Cuba to learn to be a freedom fighter. Or you want to go to Bulgaria to learn Esperanto. How will you get there?'

'I can find a job when I get there,' I said. 'Work and study.'

'And I can put my head in a bucket of water and gurgle,' he said. 'But where will that get me? You don't know how hard these things are. I asked you how will you get there?'

He looked at me expectantly but I said nothing. How did I know how I would get there? I would find a way.

He made an impatient clucking noise. 'You have to be very tough for this kind of thing,' he said.

I nodded meekly. I was relieved that he had not laughed me out of the house, or accused me of abandoning them. I suppose I had also thought that he would be angry when he found out, and I had wanted to get the unpleasantness over with. So I was prepared to listen dutifully to any advice. He grinned at me and shook his head. The dust was beginning to settle on his cuffs again. The screams of children playing outside came in through the open window. The heat was coming in waves off the whitewashed walls.

'Wait a minute,' he said.

He got up quickly and went into his bedroom. He returned with a large map of Africa. He hitched his trousers up and got down on his knees. He adjusted himself and then spread the map out in front of him.

'It's an old map,' he said, and glanced at me as if he expected me to say something. I removed from my mind the thought that he looked foolish down there, for fear that it might show in my face. He pointed decisively in the region of Lake Nyanza. *We'll make camp here and attack the enemy at dawn.* He traced a route from Kampala – who would think of going there now? – through the Bahr el Ghazal and down the Nile. I pictured myself on Cleopatra's barge, glinting with bronze and gold leaf, with its fountains and leviathan leitmotifs leaping in the equatorial sun. 'All the way to Alexandria,' he said.

He traced the route back. *Alexandria! The city of the great conqueror!* And here the Ruwenzori: two-headed Mountains of the Moon, rumbling storms in their coming. And here is Adowa where the Ethiopian monks deflowered the pride of Italy. Near the mouth of the Tana was where the Shirazi princeling, fleeing the wrath of his master, sat to wipe his arse before discovering the Blue Nile. He laughed as he mocked his own excitement.

31

'Yes, you go,' he said with a sigh as he came back to his chair. 'Show them that we're not all finished. The things they do to us in this place ... ' He leant forward and laid his hand on my thigh: 'Only one thing. Don't lose your faith in God. When you go to these foreign places ... '

He grinned and leant back. Suddenly he chuckled and shook his head: 'You're a secret one,' he said. 'Don't tell your mother. She'll start to cry or something. You leave this to me. First you need a passport. I know someone in the Immigration Department. He'll help us.' He made a sign to indicate that money would change hands. He glanced at his watch and made a face of surprise at it.

'You leave the passport to me,' he said. 'I must go now. It'll be a great journey. I wish I was young too.'

He flicked his cuffs, glanced at his watch again and left. He left me feeling more optimistic than I thought I should. It became a small conspiracy between us, and we would talk about it when we were alone. My optimism did not last. I suspected that he was playing a game with me, that his enthusiasm and tales of attempts to bribe officials were a fiction, an elaborate hoax. Sometimes a look of amused malice would pass across his face. I was reluctant to believe that he would play with me in such an elaborate and cruel way. Then one afternoon, several weeks after our first conversation, he came home from work in a terrible temper. He did not speak to anybody, but this was not unusual. Every now and again he caught my eye, and I knew that I was part of his anger in some way. I left the house and wandered the afternoon streets to keep out of his way.

I went back to the house to find him waiting for me in the guest-room. He beckoned me in as I made to walk past. He was the scowling, gruff-voiced tyrant again. It was very hot in the house, and the dust had risen from multitudinous corners so that the air rasped with grit.

'Where have you been?' he asked, the sweat standing in angry bubbles on his forehead. I saw that he had not taken his habitual shower and afternoon nap, mortifying himself into a rage. I waited in silence, hoping that he would continue talking without an answer from me, hoping that he would burst out with his grievances and anger and then leave me in peace. He scowled, waiting for an answer.

'To the docks,' I said.

'I've been waiting here,' he burst out. 'I haven't even had a wash, and you've been playing at the docks. You want this, you want that, but you want somebody else to do it for you. You don't care what humiliations you put people through. I went to all this trouble ... and you're playing in the docks.'

He stood up suddenly and I tensed, thinking that he was going to hit me. He pointed to the chair he had been sitting in, and I sat down. He paced in front of me, turning to glare at me now and then. *I'm getting tired of this*, I thought. *I'm a man now.*

'I had no one to look after me,' he said suddenly. 'I had no father. Did you know that? But you ... you expect me to see all these people, suffer all this ... disrespect. And what do you care? You go and play at the docks.'

He stood at the window, a hand gripping one of the bars. 'I spoke to the Immigration man today,' he said, speaking more softly and looking away from me. 'He told me there's a new law. He said I can't apply for a passport because I've been in prison. Did you know that I've been in prison?'

His face did not change, and the question came casually. He cleared his throat and I watched him swallow the phlegm that he had brought up. I had pictured him

33

standing in the dark of the tailor's junk-yard, the smell of rotting fruit turned sour by goat droppings and piss, while at his feet the little boy whimpered. I pictured him gloating over the shattered body: *Have you had enough?*

'It's better you should know this from me,' he said, frowning. 'I committed no crime ... but people never forget.'

The boy walks the streets now in rags, clean out of his mind. Little children taunt him and pull his trousers down for a joke and put old mango stones and bits of cassava up his anus. He was searching my face, looking for signs, looking for sympathy.

'They accused me of assaulting an eight-year-old boy,' he said through gritted teeth. 'A half-wit boy that slept in the streets.' He waited for me, but I made no sign. I knew I was rejecting an appeal but I was too young then to understand the cost of such things. He walked back to the window and stood there for a moment.

'I was innocent,' he said, looking at me with wide, appealing eyes. 'They just wanted some nobody to blame. Do you understand?'

I nodded. He sighed.

'They let me out after three months,' he said. 'That proves it, doesn't it? Then we came to live here, with thieves and prostitutes, in this dirt. These people don't forget.'

He glanced at his watch and looked out of the window, looking down the street. 'I must have a wash,' he said, sighing. 'Your mother ... she was a great comfort to me. She was beautiful. She was really beautiful,' he repeated softly. 'Did you know she was about as old as you are when I married her?'

He nodded and muttered something I did not hear. He leant against the wall, looking out of the window and saying nothing for a long time. A warm puff of air came into the room: the land breeze, slipping swiftly, bringing relief to our dusty cell. Twilight gloom was beginning to gather. He turned back to me and I saw that he was smiling.

'She was a great comfort,' he said.

A car stopped outside and hooted twice, its radio blaring. He looked out of the window and waved. 'I must change. Go and tell him to wait for a few minutes,' he told me.

She was beautiful and he turned her into a creature that lived on pain. Said, you wounded little fucker, did you know that she was a great comfort to him? Now he found his comfort where he could. I did not believe him, and I feared that the truth of what had happened did not matter any more. For as long as I had known him he had spent his nights whoring and drinking, and we all acted as if we did not know where he went while he was out. We ate and lived as if nobody was absent. And when he came home in the early hours, stumbling against the door, shouting obscene abuse, beating my mother, we all acted asleep. At times I thought I should do something to stop him. I was the eldest, and only a few inches shorter than him. Perhaps we were all as pathetic as he thought we were, but I was afraid to shame my mother. Even little Saida knew what was expected of her. Nobody had taught us to do this. We did it to save our mother from the shame that we knew she felt, and that we felt with her. In the day, nothing was said of the nights. It was as if they never happened. We did not speak of his drinking or his violence even in passing. He did not often bruise her where it showed – and even then all that we did was avoid looking at it. During the day, our father was the wrathful master, whose word had the authority of the sanction of God. I think our fear of him, and the pretence of respect, only made him loathe us more.

I wondered what he would have done if he had discovered Zakiya's pregnancy. His sense of honour would have demanded some retribution. It was what would have been expected of a father – and a brother, come to that. As it was, they kept it all from my father. Bi Mkubwa, my grandmother, took her away for a few days, to stay with a friend, she said, and Zakiya came back cleansed and chastened, at least for a while.

Zakiya had been precocious. At an early age she had abandoned her role as the household skivvy, the customary lot of the girl child. The first hints of her budding womanhood had come when she was only nine. She had then been forced into a *buibui*, the black shroud of modesty, and been forbidden to play in the streets. My grandmother started to talk about atomic bombs and men in the sky. She started talking about finding a husband and Zakiya had laughed in her face, running away from her as she tried to smack her for her disrespect. None of this was enough to suppress her obvious and aggressive charms, and she found ways of escaping the attentions of my grandmother and my mother, her chaperones. She wanted to act in a school play but my grandmother forbade it. She wanted to ride a bicycle but she was refused permission. She was told she should learn how to cook first. When she was twelve she was taken out of school, because she failed to gain a place in a government secondary school and my father did not see the point of sending her to a fee-paying school. Sometimes she borrowed my books. I remember she cried while she read *Romeo and Juliet*.

It was only later, after her pregnancy was discovered and quickly disposed of, that she told me of the man who had become her lover. He was one of the teachers at her old school, a boy from the country in his first job. He was no older than I was at the time. Zakiya said she did not know what had happened to him, and she was afraid to ask. She asked me to find out for her. I wonder now that she did not think that I would seek to protest her dishonour by taking a stick to him, or at least giving him away. I asked for her, and discovered that he had requested a transfer to the country.

They kept it from my father, but for Zakiya it was as if all self-esteem were lost. Now, at sixteen, she moved from one affair to another with the cynicism of a much older person, abandoning all discretion. As my initial shock at her behaviour lessened, I began to see the pleasure she took in what she did. In the streets she was brazen with her beauty and was proud of the admiration she aroused. In quiet moments she knew the consequences of her freedom. I tried to find a way of speaking to her, but what was there to tell her that she did not already know? That her actions were as close to self-destruction as a woman could manage? That her maddened rage would eventually leave her rejected and abused? She brushed my attempts away, and smiled with the flush of her conquests and the joy of her new powers. Her future was already mapped. Sooner or later, when times were hard enough, she would become somebody's mistress, if she was lucky.

My mother pleaded with her. Some evenings as I lay sprawled on a mat in the backyard, revising for the examinations, I heard them whispering, huddled over the light of a hurricane lamp, in another part of the yard. My mother would start to sob in her misery, and in the end Zakiya would join in. I wanted to go and be with them, but I was afraid they would reject my offer of comfort. Zakiya became something else we did not speak about.

They tried to keep all this from me because it was not the kind of thing men should involve themselves with. They were afraid of any affection I attempted to show because it made me seem soft and suspect. I had seen the suspicious glint in my grandmother's eye when I had once stroked Zakiya's hair in her presence.

The passport conspiracy between my father and me ended with our afternoon conversation. There were no more meaningful looks and whispered reports about immigration officials. I put in an official application for a passport, knowing that there was little chance of getting one. The examinations, in any case, were drawing near and overtaking all other anxieties. I spent my afternoons at school, revising and then going for exhausting runs on the track. There was contentment in the rigour of the regime. Time was accounted for and given over to one narrow purpose. I did not dwell on the futility of this labour, that our results would probably not even be published, for fear that we might decide to seek better fortunes elsewhere. At school, examination students strutted around, indulged by the teachers and held in awe by the younger boys. Our revision times were monitored by the younger boys, who created myths about our diligence, as we had done with those who had gone before us.

I came home in the early evening, and often the house was empty. My mother and Bi Mkubwa usually went visiting in the afternoon, or were attending one of the endless women's functions. Saida, my youngest sister, sometimes went with them but more often would be playing with the other children in the clearing. I would sit on my mat in the backyard, reading or leaning against the hot wall in an exhausted stupor. My grandmother liked to creep up on me when I was in such a state and say something charming and encouraging. *You'll fail*.

With the passage of years, her cruelty had become ridiculous, clownish. Nobody took any notice of her any more, and she crept round the house, all eyes and ears, alert to any disrespect. *They'll put you in a madhouse*, she liked to say. I used to think it was too cruel to laugh. Sometimes she wagged her finger at me, then retreated to her room, smacking the door against the frame before bolting it. Yet whenever she came back from the functions that they attended, she brought me a piece of cake or a sweet. *Feeding the animal*, she used to say, laughing the strained wheezing laughter of ailing lungs.

The functions and the visits were important to my mother. They were part of the respectability that my father's new job had given us. She took trouble over her clothes now, at least when she went out. And there was Zakiya to chide her into excess. *Aa-ah, don't make me ridiculous, girl*, she would say, but now she wore perfume and darkened her eyelids with kohl. She visited a dressmaker with her bundles of poplin and taffeta and silk that she had acquired from the door-to-door man. In the evenings she would change into her rags again and fuss about the yard with our supper. At the end of the long day, she said her evening prayers on a mat in the yard and then rolled over into an exhausted nap. It was then that I would hear her moaning in her sleep, while I lay a few feet away, peering at my books in the light of the oil lamp.

When she woke, after an hour or so, we talked for a while. She would ask me deliberately leading questions about school, insultingly obvious in their intent, but I could not resist showing off my knowledge. Sometimes she dozed while I talked, and I mercilessly shook her awake because I had not finished recounting the laboratory process of manufacturing chlorine or some such. I knew I had to talk to her about leaving but was always consumed with cowardice when the moment came to speak. I waited for an evening when she had not been out in the afternoon, and would not be so tired and preoccupied.

I found her in the backyard one evening when I returned from school. She was squatting on the ground, lighting the fire. I squatted near her. It seemed the wrong moment. The thought of leaving to seek a better life elsewhere had started to seem an irresponsible ambition, and in any case, unlikely to be realised. She glanced at the sky then busied herself with the pots.

'Will it rain do you think?' she asked eventually.

The skies had been gloomy for several days, and during the day the humidity was unbearable. We had had one dry storm already, when the wind had whipped the dust into angry devils that hurtled frenziedly in all directions.

'No,' I said. 'A few more days yet.'

She glanced again at the sky then looked at me.

'It will rain tonight,' she said. 'What do you know about it? All this dust and heat has been with us for such a long time. It's the season for rain now. They'll be praying for it in the country. It'll rain, I know about such things,' she said with a hint of teasing in her voice.

'What are you cooking?' I asked her.

She blinked with long-suffering slowness. Bananas again. Was it that times were that hard? She had by then lost interest in making ends meet, in producing clever meals out of tripe and sardines. On some evenings she gave us a few pennies each to go to the tea-house for some buns and beans. She accepted any complaints we made with silent and guilty resentment. She rarely ate anything herself at night, but always cooked something if my father was in. I don't think I minded the buns and beans quite as much as the bananas, and I don't think I blamed her for refusing to skivvy for the rest of us. Sometimes, though, as the heavy banana stodge rumbled its way through the coils I wondered if the money could not be better spent than on clothes and perfumes and booze.

'Are you hungry?' she asked. 'You're always hungry.'

She pulled the bunch of green bananas towards her and started breaking them off. She paused to clean something off the skin, as if it mattered. Her head was low over her work, tilted slightly towards one side. I was sorry about making her feel guilty about the food.

'I like bananas,' I said.

She looked up and smiled. *Liar!*

'Have you prayed tonight?' she asked, clicking the conversation into a different gear. 'I don't suppose you've had time. These days you're too busy to spare any time for God.' She looked again at the sky and sighed. 'They used to make sacrifices for rain. The old people in the village took rice, or flour, sometimes an animal, to the shrine on the cliff. You could hear the spirits at night. That's what we used to think when we were children, my brother and I. Sometimes we heard them walking through the village, dragging their baskets for offerings behind them. My brother wanted us to go and spend the night at the shrine, to try and see them. I told him we would be struck blind. My father said they were just savage customs.'

'Did the rains come?' I asked.

'Eh?' she asked, looking at me from a long distance. 'It'll rain tonight. Look at the sky.'

She peeled the bananas with a sharp stick and threw them into a pot of water by her feet. Every time she threw a banana in, the splash wet her feet. She did not seem to notice.

'Have you heard about bin Said?' she asked.

My resolution was weakening, and I was tempted to give up the conversation and wander the streets. She seemed so

41

vulnerable, so sad, and I was reluctant to add to her misery with talk of departure. That was the explanation I gave myself for my cowardice.

'He killed his dog today. He drove his car right over it and it popped like a tomato. I saw it, I was there. It got up and dragged itself away … '

I stood up to leave. She looked up and smiled. 'You were always soft-hearted,' she said, laughing at me.

'What will happen to him?' I asked, preparing an exit.

'They'll put him in jail,' she sneered. 'They're just like animals, his whole family. Look at the bastards they've produced between them.'

There was a rumour that bin Said had pursued my mother for years, had written letters to her – she who cannot read – which she had passed on to my father. There was good blood in bin Said. He was descended from the Busaid family, the rulers of Zanzibar until the revolution, and the sultans of Oman until this day. He was the grandson of the original slave-drivers, a man of distinction. In his youth he had terrorised the streets, and the colonial authorities had turned a blind eye to him, not wishing to damage their relations with his powerful family. He even killed a man once, an English sailor. The authorities turned a blind eye to that too. But times had changed, and bin Said had turned to having long conversations with his gin bottle and leaning out of his window shouting abuse at passers-by. His forays into the outdoors always ended with some act of unprovoked arrogance. The new authorities were still indulgent with him. They assumed he was mad and only locked him up in the madhouse overnight to calm him down.

'I'll just go out for a while,' I said.

I walked down the alley by the side of the house. The old man brothel-keeper was at his window, sitting behind the bars, looking out into the dark alley. He often did that, sitting with the window-shutters open, staring at the wall of our house. His window was at an angle to the window in my grandmother's room. His vigils angered my grandmother to distraction. At times he burnt incense, and often played bagpipe on records.

When I was a child he used to pamper me, hold me in his arms and stroke my cheeks. My mother was too afraid of him to express her horror. She warned me off him, telling me he was a dirty man, and making me swear that I would not tell him what she had said. In the end she had told my father of the old man's fondness for me. My father had ranted at me first, calling me a little whore. *What does he do? Tell me the truth!* Then he had gone round to the old man and threatened him with everything from castration to God's vengeance. He came back angry and humiliated, for the old man had not been silent and the customers had come to his aid. The old man never spoke to me after that, and I avoided the alleyway whenever I could.

As I walked past the window the old man sniggered, as he always did. Once I turned to look after I had walked past and had seen on his face a grimace of such loathing that I had never dared do it again. I dreamed of those fierce, watery eyes gazing out of the darkness of the dank alleyway.

In the clearing under the old mzambarau tree, tilly-lamps were spluttering to life as people prepared for the evening. Under one of the lamps, the interminable card game was still going on. Scattered round the edge of the clearing were the trolleys of the kabab-sellers and the peanut- and sweet-vendors. The radio of the Adusi Restaurant was blaring its mixture of songs and endless best wishes to friends and relatives. Saida came running out of the shadows and took my hand.

'Where you going?' she asked, making childish faces of pleasure at me. I did not answer but instead tried to pull the two wiry bunches of hair that thrust out on either side of her head. She beat my hands away and belted back into the knot of children from which she had appeared. She was then nearly ten years old, just the age to be hidden away from the gaze of men. It was her childishness that still saved her from that fate. She was the luckiest of us. She had always been able to withdraw herself from the turmoils at home, and always with a kind of contentment that had nothing to do with what was going on around her. My mother called her dreamy and often became frustrated with her inattention. Saida would be hurt by this, and for a day or two would remember to help with the washing. She would fold her school uniform, put her books away and offer to make people cups of tea. It would only last for a short while, then she would revert to her careless self, too preoccupied with the joy of her inner dramas to worry about being good.

The night was very quickly in control. Shadows stretched out on the road. Street-lamps glowed dimly, dotting the road through the township. Kerosene lamps threw squares of light out of barred windows. The shadows that I passed moved and flickered, staring. In the pallid glow of the lamps, the world seemed like a plain of rubble and boulders on the sea-bed – not the real world. As I walked past empty garage yards and locked-up warehouses it seemed as if I was strolling round the abandoned camp fires of a great host ... a place that had been arbitrarily and expediently picked for a bivouac on the road to other places. I caught sight of a fleeting image of a half-clad girl, moving away into the early evening shadows. Her head swayed grace-fully as she hurried, her step so certain.

I re-entered the clearing from the opposite end, by the Adusi Restaurant. It was bathed in light. The sign-post above the entrance was covered with insects that whirred frantically for a touch of the lamps. Outside the restaurant a man was standing behind an aluminium-topped table making chapatis. Round the corner from the restaurant was a long, narrow alleyway, where customers went to relieve swollen bladders. At the end of the alleyway was the branch office of our People's Progressive Party. Daubed in black paint above the doorway were the words FREEDOM NOW. The lettering was inelegant, done in the heat of the struggle. It was faded now, a leftover from a time when such slogans had meaning.

The office was crowded with people playing card games and draughts. In the inner office, the chairman of the branch was holding court, sipping coffee out of a tiny cup and listening to the animated sycophancy around him. He was one of the new men. He represented us at the councils of the notables and the powerful. We had already learnt not to choose one of ourselves for such tasks, not one of those who had for centuries, and against all visible evidence, persisted in calling themselves Arabs. Independence had taught us enough of the violent hatred that the rest of the country felt for the history that we had been part of. We had strutted our miscegenated way through the centuries, making monkeys out of our half-brothers and half-sisters, while those that we claimed to be part of, where they knew of us, disclaimed and despised us as some bastard offspring of energetic and uncouth sons. So now we chose a chairman who did not speak like us, and magnanimously, did not speak too often against us. He was the only person who could persuade the hospital to send an ambulance if somebody was seriously ill. He could, with a few whispered words, persuade a policeman from an excess of zeal. He could put in the decisive word for the student who looks to have failed his exams, or for the business man who seems certain to lose his licence. So he was paid court, and languidly accepted the homage. The walls of his office were covered with slogans, and photographs of the party notables. There was a large photograph of our Leader, embarrassingly fat and with eyes hooded with malice and booze, standing next to the Queen of England.

It had been different during the struggle to rid ourselves of the British. We had then revelled in our oneness, speaking words of tolerance for past wrongs, forgiving ourselves for the horrors of our history and fooling only ourselves. We had stormed the streets in excitement and delight, yelling the pleasure of our approaching freedom. We became frantic with patriotic joy in the days leading up to independence. I remember a man wandering the streets playing a saxophone, and all the children followed him round the town singing his tune. *Voti mpeni jogoo*. There were torch-lit school demonstrations, athletics meetings, sports tournaments … and the whole nation was on the march. It was like nothing we had ever seen before. The new riot-police, brought into being by the pre-independence caretaker government, was rehearsing for the parade. Fishermen were cleaning and painting their boats, making ready for the boat race. PWD workers were making floats for the costume parade. Neighbourhoods were putting the final touches to their carnival acts. Boy Scouts were out camping, refining the skills they would display, practising their battle-cries: *kaliba kaliba yahoo!* And at school we were asked to write an essay entitled: *What Independence Means to Me*. A jamboree!

Now we are free. Our leader stands next to the Queen of England with no loss of face. He is obese, filled to bursting with the rotten fruit of his power: corrupt, debauched and obscene. He is protected by the riot-police, which has now grown into an army with tanks and machine-guns, and which only has one enemy. Soldiers don't have to knock any more before they enter a house.

I stopped at the cinema to look at the stills. *My Fair Lady* had been retained for the third consecutive week, playing to full houses. I took a step back to get a better view and bumped into a man standing behind me. I turned to look, words of apology leaping to my mouth. I could not speak. The man looked calmly back at me. I mumbled something and walked away, surprised by the fear I had felt. I turned to look, and the man was still standing there, looking after me.

I heard the muadhin calling people to prayers. I followed, impelled by a need for communion. I washed at the water tanks, glancing into the concrete trough to see if the frayed tooth-brush was still there. The water ran off my hands and fell in a torrent into the slimy gutter. The latrine was at one end of the wash-room, and a man was coughing vigorously in there, covering up the noise of his ablutions.

I said the proper words out of habit, marvelling none the less at the sense of cleansing I felt. There was a calmness in the mosque that made the heart feel that here all its rackings could come to rest. The congregation buzzed gently as it murmured private prayers. Then one man near the front stood up and walked towards the alcove that faced Makka. He raised his hands in the air, spoke the *nua* and led the rest of us in prayer. At the end we all shook hands with our neighbours. I moved from my place in the line and went to sit at the back of the mosque, relishing the gloom and the congregation's measured chants of praise to the prophet.

I walked to the junction of Kisa Street, and wondered whether I should continue or turn homewards. A man came out of one of the houses. He looked at me cautiously and then smiled as if he had recognised me. He was a short man, tubby and genial, his trousers well down his belly.

'Are you lost?' he asked.

'No,' I said. 'I'm just on my way home.'

'Don't hang around the streets then,' he said, a subtle unease behind his genial voice. 'Aren't you afraid? Are you mad?'

When I walked back past the Adusi Restaurant, the old man himself was at the table by the door. Juma Adusi worked in the kitchens at the busiest hours, and then came out later in the evening to count the money. He had a reputation for meanness and his appearance did nothing but enhance it. He was thin and always dressed in rags. His hands were disfigured by taut patches of skin that were hideously pink and raw. His customers endlessly speculated on the hoard he had hidden somewhere.

The benches outside the restaurant were crowded with people listening to the news on the radio. Among them were the serious students of world affairs. They had left their homes to come and listen to the news in this nightly observance. They sipped their coffee in silence and exchanged glances as conspiracies revealed themselves in the newscaster's words. When the bulletin ended, they unfurled their theories on the true state of affairs. Soon enough, the point at issue became one of the few things they really cared about: the Arab–Israeli wars.

It was agreed to be beyond argument that Israel did not win the Six-Day War on her own. One man claimed to know that Adolf Hitler was the *rais* of Israel, and that King Hussein had sold him the battle plans. The general opinion was that the Egyptians were winning in Sinai. They had the Israelis caught in a pincer movement, and were drawing them farther and farther in before slamming the door and annihilating them. With victory in the grasp of the Arabs, the Americans intervened. The Russians, who had promised to help the Arabs, did nothing. Instead of dropping an atomic bomb on America, they made speeches at the United Nations. The subject was full of variations, and some very strong views were held, but on the whole the view prevailed that it was these bombs that were responsible for giving little girls big breasts.

I found my mother stretched out on the mat in the yard. The lamplight softened the contours of her face, fleshing the bones to fullness. As I approached, my movements disturbed her and she jerked suddenly awake.

'It's all right,' I said, crouching down beside her. 'It's all right ... but you'd better go inside. I think it'll rain at last.'

She sat up slowly, grimacing with pain. She massaged the shoulder she had been lying on, tried to stifle a yawn and failed. The lamplight threw ugly shadows on her face as her mouth yawed for air. I sat behind her and kneaded her shoulders, pressing with the palm of the hand as she had taught me. She shook her shoulders to dismiss me and smiled as I came to sit opposite her. 'Where have you been?' she asked. 'You should be revising for your examinations. And you haven't even eaten your supper yet.'

'Was the meat all right? You said it smelt a bit bad.'

'If you buy cheap meat you can always smell the saving that you've made. Ask your father about it, not me.'

'I talked to him about leaving,' I said. 'After the examinations ... '

She waited for me, then nodded.

'I have to think about that,' I said. 'He told me about the prison ... why they sent him.'

49

She hissed in alarm and put her finger across her lips. 'Not so loud!'

'How old was he?' I asked in a whisper.

She did not reply for a while. When she looked up there was guilt and fear in her eyes. 'It wasn't his fault. They just wanted somebody to accuse. He would not have done that. You must believe me.'

She looked at me as if she had wronged me. *Yes*, I said to comfort her. 'You could have been a better son to him,' she said. 'You could have helped him more.'

That accusation caused me pain. I remembered the time of Said's funeral, and how my father had tearfully accused me of Said's death. Somebody had picked me up and whisked me away, and spoke kindly to me and made me ashamed of my father. Who could think to blame him for the death of his first-born?

'Perhaps,' I said. 'But perhaps there was nothing I could do to help him.'

'Don't say that,' she said, looking down.

'Was that when he started drinking? When he came out?'

'You don't know the things that happened,' she said finally. 'The things they did to him … When he came out he was different. You and Said were just little babies. It was then he started drinking. It wasn't his fault. They hurt him. I mean they beat him. They broke his heart.'

'He goes out to women … and he beats you.'

She shut her eyes and then sighed. She bent down to adjust the lamp, lowering her head towards the light so that her face seemed burnished with a metallic hardness.

'You want your father to be a monster, don't you? Don't you understand? He finds things very hard. It was all too much for him … the prison and Said.'

'He still beats you,' I said.

'What do you want me to do?' she shouted. 'Why are you like this?' She glared at me for a moment. She sighed, then smiled. 'Playing the hero now. You shouldn't take any notice of the things I say. I thank God for a son like you. Just ignore the old woman.'

'You're not old.'

'I feel old,' she said.

'It's the grey hair,' I said. 'I'll buy you some dye and show you how young you look.'

'Don't you dare,' she said, grinning. 'People will think I've got a man after me.' She hauled herself to her feet, groaning and muttering about children who wandered the streets until all hours of the night as if they did not have a home. I did not like the sound of that *children* but I let it pass. She went into the tiny shed that served as our pantry and came out with the cooking pot that contained the remains of the bananas.

'They're making a lot of noise,' she said. Sounds of drunken revelry came from the old man's brothel. Somebody was laughing hysterically to the sound of bagpipe music. I nodded, addressing myself to a stodgy lump of congealed banana. She watched me struggle for a while, looking at me with increasing astonishment. 'Get a glass of water before you choke,' she said.

I went to the tap and cupped my hands under it, pouring the water into my mouth. I felt the heaviness sink lower into my stomach. Dutifully I went back to the pot. A strong breeze suddenly picked up and the lamp guttered. I sensed her looking up as well.

'There'll be rain tonight,' she said.

'Yes,' I said.

'God has mercy.'

She took the pot from me when I could eat no more. She ran some water into it and left it to soak overnight. 'So what will you do?' she asked when she came back.

'I want to study … but the problem is money.' There was a sudden yelp in the darkness, and a dog scurried across the yard, disappearing into the shadows. 'Maybe I should just try to get a job.'

'I think we can find the money,' she said. 'If you know what you want to do.'

Yes mummy. I smiled at her, determined to be tolerant of her maternal optimism. Where there is a will there is a way and all that crap. She grinned as she divined my thought, and for a moment looked really happy.

'Your uncle Ahmed in Nairobi, my brother,' she said. 'We'll go to him. He's a rich man now. You're his family. He must help you.'

'Very funny. You're making a joke.' Although I had not really expected her to come up with anything astonishing, I was still disappointed that Uncle Ahmed was all that she could think of.

'Who's joking?' she asked, laughing. 'He owes me money. When our father died, your uncle Ahmed sold the shop and the business and kept everything. He told me if I ever needed money I could go to him. He robbed me to make himself rich, so now we'll take it back.'

'And how are you going to get it back? Steal it?'

'We could,' she said, still laughing. 'Well, we can try anyway. What's the matter with you? It's a chance.'

'Ma, what kind of chance. He doesn't even know you exist any more. He doesn't write to you, he doesn't even send word to you.'

'It's a chance,' she repeated stubbornly. 'You must go and see him in Nairobi. I'll tell your father to write to him and explain. He'll be difficult, your father I mean, but he'll do it. Then you go to Nairobi … '

'And Uncle Ahmed will find me irresistible.'

She pealed with laughter. 'He'll like you. I know Ahmed … he likes people to look him in the face and tell him what they want.'

'I've come for my mother's money,' I offered.

She slapped me on the knee. 'Go to sleep now. I'll talk to your father tomorrow. And you must revise hard and pass your examinations. Every night you disappear, when I ask where you've been you say you've been for a walk. You'll bring a pregnant girl home one of these days.'

Yes mummy … me big bush-goat. In the gloom I sensed her settling herself back on the mat, waiting for my father to return.

I slept on a mattress in the corridor. During the day the bundle of *kapok* was stuffed into the space under the food cupboard. At night I drew it out, complete with the rag that served for bedding, and stretched out on it. I turned myself round to try and read by the light of the electric bulb in the corridor. Three of the rooms in the house had been electrified, but we were only allowed weak bulbs, unless we had visitors.

Around me were signs of ruin. The floor was pockmarked, the concrete perished. The whitewashed walls were smeared with grease. The food cupboard was infested with cockroaches, and at night they came out foraging, roaming the house and the yard at will. My nightmare was being woken up by the feel of their rasping claws on my face. For years I had lived with this filth, but now it was difficult to do the simplest thing without worrying about it. I had to work myself up into a state to enter the bathroom, where a green slime grew all over the floor. The walls in the pantry were covered with the spores of black fungus, and filthy skeins of old spider webs trailed across the ceiling beams. Zakiya complained bitterly about the filth but always declined my mother's invitation to do something about it. None of us did anything about it.

Every night the mosquitoes came. With unerring cruelty they came for the tender skin of the ear. Even though I slept with the sheet over my head, I could not escape the feeling that their long-stemmed mouths were puncturing the sheet and drinking my blood.

Those last days before the exams were filled with anxieties about failure and with dreams of Uncle Ahmed's largesse. There had already been casualties among the students, some of whom would go down in legend as having worked too hard or taken too many stimulants to keep themselves awake. On the eve of the exams I could not sleep. I could hear my mother out in the yard. My father was still out.

There was a moment when I thought I was still dreaming, but the blows on my shoulder were real enough. It was a slow process to drag myself from the clarity of the dream to the confusion lowering over me.

'Come outside,' whispered my mother.

I followed her out, anticipating something to do with my father. The street-lamp threw a diffused glow across the yard, not enough to illuminate anything but sufficient to scatter the pitch-darkness of the night. A man coughed in the darkness and panic leaped through my mind. My mother was fumbling with the lamp. Eventually she struck a match, and the flame lit up her cowering body and flooded the space around her with light.

'Who's there?' I asked. I tried to remove any challenge from my voice because I was certain it was my father looming in the shadows. A prolonged giggle was the only answer I received.

'Step into the light,' my mother said, her voice trembling.

The man sighed but did not move. As my mother moved the lamp nearer to him, I saw that it was Khamis, one of my father's friends. He was leaning against the corner of the house, one foot in the yard, the other in the alley. He made an effort to lever himself off the wall but gave up with a sigh. 'You must come,' he said.

He closed his eyes and did not seem inclined to elaborate. I went back for my clothes and hurried out half-dressed. Khamis was on the ground, his head hidden by the corner of the house.

'Did he say where he is?' I asked my mother.

She shrugged and pointed at Khamis. *Ask him*. His eyes were closed but he was smiling contentedly. He was only a slight man and it was quite easy to drag him up. He responded limply, and I understood the temptation to hit and hurt people in such a state. He smelt of something rotten, something abandoned. He growled cheerfully when he recognised me. He swayed in front of me, eyes closed again.

'Where is he?' I asked.

He shook his head as if he was having trouble understanding. 'He's making trouble,' he said, speaking with a struggle. He sounded as if he was talking with his mouth full. 'He wants to fight. He'll be beaten. He's drunk.'

He said the last word with loathing, then chortled and slapped his forehead at the absurdity of it all. He shook his head again and began to cry. My mother pushed me aside and slapped Khamis across the face. I pushed her back. Khamis was now sobbing like a child.

'Where is he?' I asked him again. I held him across the shoulders to stop the wild rocking that accompanied his sobs.

'At Sood's,' he cried, his voice small like a child's.

'I'd better go,' I said to my mother. Her face was hard with anger. She seemed to be waiting for me to say something, to gloat or complain.

'Do you know what time it is? You have an examination tomorrow.'

'Yes, I know, but I have to go.'

Khamis groaned and pushed my hand away as I went to help him off the wall. The sight of my mother, holding a jagged piece of firewood, alarmed him enough to move. He staggered ahead of me, muttering and spitting. I left him in the clearing. When he realised what I was saying, he allowed himself to slide to the ground with relief. I was tempted to search him, to see if he had any money. I had heard stories of fat wallets found in the pockets of sleeping drunks. Khamis farted loudly and without warning. I hurried away as he strained to repeat the performance.

It was a dark night. The emptiness was eerie. There was a touch of dampness in the atmosphere, a tang in the air. The rains had started, but only in a desultory, tentative way. Any day the real rains would start. I reached the sea front and followed the old cobbled pavement that ran all the way to the docks. The hissing of the sea drowned the frightening sound of my footsteps. Customs guards were lounging near the dockyard gate. I thought they would stop me, but they stared blankly and left me alone. A footpath ran alongside the wire fence that skirted the dock area. I passed pyramids of sacks and crates. We had played here as children, making hide-outs and caves.

The path branched away from the fence and headed towards the warehouses that now stood silent and huge in the emptiness of the night. Beyond the warehouses was a grotto of mango trees. In the clearing between the two stood an old, low building, surrounded by pieces of junk that had been salvaged from elsewhere and dragged here. This was Sood's, dirty and disreputable, tolerated by the law because it attracted those whom events had already defeated.

Two men were lounging on the steps. They stirred as they saw me approach. As I came nearer, I saw them relaxing again, smiles on their faces. I stopped some distance from the steps. One of them, the man wearing a sleeveless shirt open to his navel, moved forward. The other man looked older. He leant against the wall, stroking his patchy beard. They both looked tough and unpleasant men, grizzled by a lifetime of living hand to mouth. The man who had moved forward tilted his head, pointing his chin at me.

'I've come for my father,' I said humbly. 'I think he's in there.'

They both laughed. I suppose it sounded childish. The older man moved quickly, rattling down the steps. I stepped back, legs tensed for flight, heart hammering. He stopped suddenly and I realised that I had raised both my fists. He eyed my fists and smiled, flicking a hand at them.

'You fuck off home before I stuff your little penis in your mouth,' he said. 'Come on, before I change my mind. Bloody swine! Get out of here.'

I lowered my arms slowly, as if I was having an internal argument about the wisdom of such leniency. The younger man laughed, then beckoned his friend. A fit of shaking passed through my limbs. The younger man spoke angrily and abusively at his companion, calling him a shit-eater and a cannibal. 'He's come to get his father,' he said. 'You don't know what that means, never having had one. Leave the boy alone.' To my eyes now he seemed a kindly man, a noble savage. 'There's no one in there,' he said, addressing me. 'He might be over there, in that junk. Now fuck off out of here, huh?'

He nodded his head once and winked. I tried to spot a human form among the old car seats and broken bed frames. There was enough light to see by, but the shadows confused the landscape. I found him lying in a boxed settee whose stuffing had been removed.

I thought at first that he was hurt. His legs were splayed out at odd angles. The arm of the settee hid the light from his face. I touched him on the arm, tentatively, but he did not move. He was still wearing his jacket, and his walking-stick was leaning against the settee as if someone had carefully placed it there. I tried to shake him awake. *Fuck my arse*, he shouted, rousing himself into a thrashing of arms and legs. I leaned forward and slapped him as hard as I could, and felt a tingle of cruel pleasure from the pain that I knew I was inflicting on his senseless body. I hit him again, feeling shame for the pleasure that it gave me. He groaned.

'Come on,' I shouted, 'It's time to go home.'

I shook him violently. He thrashed out again and this time landed a blow on my chest. Then he saw me. He struggled to a sitting position, as if trying to hide his drunkenness. He leant back with a groan, smiling mockingly at me. 'You see how I am,' he drawled.

There was a noise behind me, and I turned to see a man crawling out of a steel drum lying on its side. He smelled of urine. 'I'm a tough guy,' he muttered as he crawled on all fours.

'I fucked his arse many times,' my father said, pointing his stick at him. 'He falls down in the streets and little children fuck him.'

The man slowly subsided, sinking flat on the ground. My father leant forward and spat at him. It did not seem to matter. The man sniggered and rolled over, suddenly looking very vulnerable. My father felt this and struggled to his feet, changing his grip on the walking-stick. I put an arm around him to shield him from the man. The touch of him was disgusting, flabby and loose. He directed us towards the man who now seemed asleep. Suddenly, with unexpected strength, my father leant forward and swung the walking-stick onto the man's back. I let go of him. He struggled to regain his balance, took a sudden breath and threw up.

I waited until he had finished, waited while he groaned and wiped himself, and only went to him when he seemed ready to go to sleep again. It took me a long time to persuade him to move and we made slow progress. It started to rain as we walked across the clearing. There were only a few drops at first, heavy and separate, landing on the skin with a squelch. It was the start of the big rains. I could tell by the size of the drops. The rain was getting heavier by the minute, spitting dust at our feet. Soon it was pounding furiously on our heads, exhilarating in its violence. We stumbled towards the shelter of a warehouse. A great sheet of water surrounded our narrow cover, pouring off the gutterless roof. I could hear my father breathing heavily next to me.

'They'll be dancing in the country,' I told him. 'Assuming you're interested ... or care.'

'Fuck off,' he mumbled.

I groped for him in the dark and found his arm. I yanked it and set off. He came without protest. The lumps of water stung as they pitted the flesh, and I felt his arm slip out of my grasp. I swiped around me but I had lost him. *The stupid bugger. I'll fail my exams.* Ahead were the Customs gates, and the lamps on either side of them were throwing wide refracted beams on the ground. I yelled out for him, hoping he would hear me above the rumble of the water. *Ba, where are you? Ba!* A song answered me, or it may have been a scream of delight. I ran towards the light, hoping that I would not collide with one of the rusty skeletons on the waste ground. I saw the wire in time to break my rush with outstretched arms. A cry came from behind me and I yelled out where I was. When I saw him he was grinning, his arms open to embrace the water that was sheeting all around us. I reached for his shoulder and pulled him towards me. He huddled to me, reciting in a whisper lines from the Koran.

The path was now very slippery and we had to walk with care. At last we reached the metal road, the refracted beams travelling far ahead of us to light our way. My father was absorbed by the sight of the rain falling across the beams of light. I started to jog away, to encourage him to follow but he called out for me to slow down. 'It won't hurt you,' he shouted. I walked ahead of him, anticipating his every movement forward, and having to go back often to persuade him to hurry. The rain had cleared his head a little and he was not staggering and falling as much as when we started out. He turned to look at the light once more, walking backwards. He toppled over very gently, as if he was carefully letting himself fall on a bed. He lay in the puddles of water, clapping his hands and laughing.

'A long time ago,' he sang, making his voice deep and croaky like an ancient sheikh reading the *tajwid*. 'When I was only a baby. And sailed the seas, searching for my *rizki*. Our ship was sunk by a reef, and we swam to the land of Socotra. The king there held us captives ... '

'You haven't been anywhere to be sunk,' I said, bending down to him and offering an arm.

He looked at me for a moment, still grinning and blinking the rain out of his eyes. 'Once upon a time,' he said, waving an oratorical finger, 'I was a man of honour. Do you know what happened?'

'Let's go home,' I said. 'Come on, old man. I've got an examination tomorrow.'

'They know about you,' he said quietly. 'I've told everybody that you're going to run away.' He held on to my arm while I pulled him up. 'You dirty bloody traitor!' he screamed at me. We walked in silence along the waterfront, stopping only once for my father to urinate. We were nearly home when he drew alongside and leaned on my arm.

'This is the best place for you,' he whispered. 'I told everybody that you're going to run away. They'll put you in prison, you fucking traitor. You're too good for us, anybody can see that. They'll put you in prison.'

'It doesn't matter,' I said, meaning that the authorities knew that I wanted to leave. I had applied for a passport.

'My dear son, my brave young genius,' he said in a high-pitched voice of mockery. 'You're afraid of nothing. What a son! Who hates his father and his mother and his people and his God ... ' I could see the hate on his face. Water was dripping off his hair. We were in the open ground under the mzambarau tree. The rain was beginning to slacken. He let go of my arm and walked away, meandering across the clearing. He stopped in front of the old man's brothel and blew an enormous raspberry at it. He waited for me to catch up, and then let me pass. He poked me in the back with his walking-stick, once, twice. I let him go first into the alley. I heard him curse as he slipped. I stepped over the half-prone body and turned into the backyard.

I started to undress while I was still outside. He appeared round the corner, his shadow looming and wavering in the darkness. My mother appeared at the door, holding a lamp above her head. She looked at me first, running her eyes the full length of my sodden, half-naked body. I smiled at her appraisal, and that seemed to reassure her, for she nodded and swung the lamp towards my father. His eyes were closed and his clothes were covered with mud. She put the lamp down by the door and went back inside. He staggered after her, rumbling with suppressed laughter.

3

The days of the examinations passed in a blur. We all recognised them as the climax of years of misery, not only because we recognised them as the threshold of whatever futures we desired for ourselves, but also because each of us hoped through them to state our worth and value. Everything conspired to seduce us into this absurd position. We were the heroes of the day, confronting the tests of life and intellect, grappling with an irrational enemy that sought at every turn to ambush and trick us. After each sitting, we set off from the examination hall in a body, like guerrillas returned from battle, wandering the streets and parading ourselves as the smiling survivors of the examiners' wiles. We formed self-important discussion groups by the roadside: should the answer have been stalactites or stalagmites? Nobody laughed at us, although our teachers feigned amusement at our intensity. We all knew the prizes that had become available to those who had succeeded ahead of us.

Our reverence for the power of these things was by then a matter of habit. Rumours had started even before the examinations were finished that the results would never be released. The government was concerned that successful students would want to leave, and with so many people leaving already, a serious shortage of teachers and penpushers was developing. There were rumours that results would only be released to those who completed two years of a new National Service. In the throes of the examinations, my interest in these things was lively but detached. They were part of the heady atmosphere of intrigue and politics and revenge that independence had brought.

It was after the relief of the examinations had subsided, and the weeks of waiting turned into months, that the meaning of what we had been denied became clear. In small numbers at first, students were called to government ministries and offered clerical jobs at reduced salaries. Others were called to the Ministry of Education and offered teaching assistantships without salaries, only expenses and the promise of a scholarship abroad when the results became known. The rest of us were advised to join the army. I went to the Immigration Office to enquire after my passport. It was a way of passing the time. I joined the queue and shuffled for hours to the counter, where the officer would tell me, without needing to consult a file, that there was nothing yet.

My father often talked to me during the long months of waiting. It was as if coming home with him that night had lifted some of the burden of dissembling off him. He wrote the letter to my uncle, a long, whining appeal to the big man. He read it to me before he sent it, drawing my attention to this or that bit of cleverness. He read it with a flourish, giving it in voice and gesture the force that it lacked on paper. He reminded Uncle Ahmed of his promise to my mother, *your dear sister*, that should she need the money from her share of the shop it would always be available. Now her son was ready to do honour to the family name, so could he please cough up? It was signed *Your Brother*.

Nearly four months passed before we received a reply. In that time it was dangerous to mention the subject of the letter in front of my father. It only brought on one of his rages. When a reply came it was vague and full of courteous address, inviting me to go to Nairobi for a holiday. This was enough for my father. He stopped cursing Uncle Ahmed as a sin-eating miser and no longer prayed that God would bring down a plague of boils on the thief. He assumed that the matter was resolved. The money was more or less on the way. *You can't expect him to say yes, I'll give you the money. It wouldn't be polite. This is enough.* He suggested that we go out and celebrate.

Sometimes he joked about the night we had come home together, telling me in a whisper how drunk he had been although I had not noticed. He told me how tired he had been that night, because he had spent the evening doing naughty things which a young man should not need to have spelt out for him. I laughed, as was expected of me.

In the house I was now referred to sarcastically as *the man going to Nairobi*. My mother bought the odd thing from the door-to-door man because she thought it would be useful on the journey to Nairobi, or Uncle Ahmed would like it as a present. Nobody mentioned the passport. Uncle Ahmed had fixed the holiday for June, two months after the arrival of his letter. I made daily visits to the Immigration Office, shuffled in the queue all day and received the same reply.

One evening, when I was beginning to despair of making the journey at all, Zakiya called me outside. She walked towards the shadows beyond the stand-pipe in the yard and waited for me there.

'I can talk to somebody,' she said. 'About the passport ... if you want me to.' I could not see her face but heard the shame in her voice. I had not realised that things had come to such a pass. The question that leapt to my mouth was *Who?* but I managed to stop myself asking it.

'No, it's all right. They'll give it to me in the end. I'll just keep on going there until they give it to me ... '

She chuckled, but it was a sad, self-pitying sound. 'You're such a child sometimes,' she said. 'I shouldn't have bothered asking you.'

'Zakiya ... '

'No, don't start,' she said sharply. 'You wouldn't even know what you were talking about. I'm seeing the man anyway ... and I thought I would ask him for you. But if you don't want me to ... '

We stood in silence for a long while. I did not know what to say to her. I think she was waiting for temptation to work on me, and I was trying to think of a way of not hurting her by my refusal. Not for a moment was I about to accept a favour from a brute who was already abusing my sister.

'I was just trying to help,' she said eventually.

I heard her swallow, trying not to cry. She had only just reached her seventeenth year. She strode back towards the house. I called to her but she ignored me.

The days dragged by slowly now. The rains had come and gone, and the dry season had returned. Weeds and bushes were everywhere in bloom, anxious to fulfil their purpose before the sun reduced them to ashes.

The old man brothel-keeper had bought himself a he-goat. He kept it tied up in the alleyway between our houses and rarely fed it. Demented with hunger and flies, it charged anything that moved within its compass. It had destroyed all the weeds within reach of its long rope, plants that for years had tenaciously clung to the walls. Sometimes, in sheer desperation, it ate mouthfuls of dirt.

The goat came to occupy an important place in our home. My mother wondered aloud whether the goat had been acquired to add variety to the orgies in the brothel. *He sits there and watches the animal starving. What is he keeping it for? It can't be for food.* My grandmother gave up everything else and devoted her waking hours to watching the hated animal. She sat by her window, trying to beat down the goat's stare with her will. My father, against whom the goat had developed an instinctive dislike, harangued it with abuse. Sometimes he marched down the dark alleyway clutching the kitchen knife, which he would brandish threateningly at the goat, swearing at it under his breath. The goat would be frantically trying to break its rope so it could charge him.

The old man was highly gratified by all this. He sat by his window, looking out on the alleyway, watching the bleating, angry goat with patient interest. My grandmother took to collecting her own urine and storing it in a bucket under her bed. Once a day she took her bucket into the alleyway and hurled the pungent fluid at the goat. As a variation, she sometimes filled thick paper bags with urine and threw them at the animal.

Neither hunger nor persecution diminished the goat's ferocity. It charged whoever was mad enough to walk through the urinous alleyway. My father was the last to give up, feeling that a matter of manly pride was involved. At his moment of defeat, he claimed that he had seen the old man on his hands and knees between the goat's legs. *What were you doing there, you old pervert? Milking it?* Children in the neighbourhood began to take an interest. My father became a figure of such ridicule that some of it began to rebound on Saida, who stayed at home to escape the teasing. Zakiya kept herself apart from all this, too caught up in her stews of passion, her reputation for promiscuity giving her now a kind of glamour.

She was above an interest in a feud with a goat. The children brought the goat what food they could, and spent hours sitting watching it in its darkened shrine. My grandmother, her progress towards senility vastly accelerated, switched her malice to the children. She rushed out when they were well-settled and dispersed them with her bucket of potent water.

It was no longer possible to hide Zakiya's activities from my father. He never spoke to Zakiya now, never looked at her. We feared for the day when he would lose restraint and assault her in one of his lunatic rages. It was as if some madness had got into her. She was unapproachable. Since I refused her offer of help she avoided me. She shut my mother up without mercy as soon as she started. As if afraid to pause, she hurled herself into squalid and open affairs with men of horrific reputation. She watched our family's feud with the goat in awed disbelief.

I was bored. I was fed up with my daily journeys to the Immigration Office. I was tired of reading the same books and walking the same routes. The dreaded Ramadhan was approaching, with its daily hungers and slow daylight hours. When it came, the whole town ground to a drowsy pace, shops shut and people slept through as much of the day as they could, fighting hunger with oblivion. When night came, life started again with a kind of abandon and frenzy. We bloated ourselves with food we had spent the day dreaming about. People roamed the streets in search of excitement and stayed out until the early hours. Children played marathon games of hide-and-seek or cops-and-robbers. It was the time for long conversations, stretching far into the night, for endless card games, for courtship. It was the daylight hunger that made it a time of pain. God had intended the rigours of

Ramadhan to teach us self-discipline, but instead tempers were on a short fuse during the day and excess followed self-denial every night.

I stayed away from the Immigration Office for the first few days of Ramadhan, while my body accustomed itself to going without food. When I reached the counter, the clerk smiled to see me again and shook his head.

'I want to see the Immigration Officer,' I said, and without waiting for a reply I lifted up the counter-flap and marched on. The clerk made no move to stop me. He leant against the counter watching me negotiate the desks as I wound towards the office. I knew exactly where it was, had seen the man come in and out countless times. I knocked on the door and entered. His name was Omar Shingo. At one time he had been a famous footballer, now he was better known for his debauches. I launched without preamble, without even looking at him, into an angry complaint. He tried to stop me once or twice: *Who are you? Go back to the counter. Where do you think you are?* I brushed him aside, and I would have hit him with something if he had tried to have me thrown out. As I focused on his smug, wasted face, I became convinced that he was the man Zakiya had in mind when she offered help.

'Have a seat,' he said at last, smiling in defeat.

'I don't want a seat. I want my passport. I've been coming here every day ... '

'I know, I know,' he said, raising a hand to silence me. 'Tell me your name and I'll get your file.'

I watched his face as I told him. He scribbled it down and went away. When he came back he was smiling. 'I know your family,' he said. 'How's your father these days? And the rest of your family?' He signed the papers in front of me and told me to give the file back to the clerk on my way out. He could not resist gloating in the end. 'Give my regards to everybody,' he said. 'And your sisters.'

It took another three weeks before the passport was ready, on the eve of Idd. The old man had his goat butchered for Idd and sent a leg round to my mother. While everybody celebrated with songs the end of Ramadhan and the arrival of the new year, I nursed the revival of my hopes as I leafed through my new passport. In the general joy of the day, Zakiya forgot herself enough to allow one of her lovers to drive her home. My father was at home, entertaining a distant relative from Tanga to a little *halwa* and coffee. When the guest left, and my father had seen him off to the bus stop, he came hurrying back to the house, in a terrible rage. My mother met him at the door and took upon her shoulders the brunt of his fury. I stood nearby, determined to intervene should he attempt to hit either of them. Zakiya sat in grandmother's room, her eyes blank with despairing indifference, looking more abandoned than any tears or screams would have made her seem. In the hallway my father swore, solemnly, calling in the name of God that all should witness this act, that should his child Zakiya not mend her ways, he would – *Wallahi Billahi* – hurl her out in the streets to fend for herself.

My mother screamed at him, begging him to take his oath back, asking him if he knew that by that oath he had turned his daughter into a street whore. My father looked at her, his rage now turning into tears. *We have done our best*, he said.

The journey to Nairobi was beginning to seem very close. My mother tried to give me as much information as she could about Uncle Ahmed. She told me about the journey. She thought herself an expert on this, having done the journey once. This was enough, for no one in the house had travelled more than thirty miles inland from the coast. She had alarming stories to tell. She told me of the discomfort of train travel, and of the drinking habits of train drivers. She told me of muggers and pickpockets who lurked at every street corner in Nairobi. She instructed me on the best way of greeting my uncle, and on what clothes would be appropriate for the cold climate there.

My grandmother watched and listened with ill-concealed disapproval. Sometimes, unable to contain her irritation with the fuss that was being made of me, she would ask how I had done in the examinations. It was her mad way of mocking us for counting our chickens. Without the goat, her days were empty now.

My mother had no doubt that Uncle Ahmed would provide the money. I told her that her share of the shop would not be enough to pay for the journey, that I would only get enough money from Uncle Ahmed if I were able to touch his goodwill. She waved my caution aside. She convinced me in the end. It seems foolish now that I should have allowed this, but the cumulative effect of our fantasies had convinced all of us that we could not be wrong.

A new law was passed that month, formalising what was already the practice, that jobs and school places would be allocated in quotas, according to the racial distribution in the population. To facilitate this, all citizens were to register their race at a new Department of Population. They would be issued with an identity pass stating name, age, address and race. Failure to produce this pass on request would lead to immediate arrest.

Consternation spread among a people whose race had become more a state of mind than any identifiable characteristic. Refusal to answer questions about race had been an act of defiance against the British, an assertion of unity and nationhood. Refusal to answer the question now was against the law. When I went to register for my card, I gave a false name. It was a useless act of defiance, but we had not at that time realised the firmness with which the government intended to deal with the problem of its mixed community. It turned out that my small act of sabotage had the potential to cause me great difficulty. No official business could be conducted without a card. The thought of the danger I was running carrying a bogus pass spoiled many quiet moments.

On the last Sunday before I left for Nairobi I was forced to use the card. Every Sunday the entire population of the town was expected to volunteer for work on the new blocks of flats that were part of the government's slum-clearance scheme. We had already successfully completed the new Party headquarters in this way. Hundreds of people turned up on the first Sunday, too afraid not to, and remembering the violence with which Youth Leaguers had ejected, people from homes and cafés and cinemas. That was for the Party Headquarters, a national priority. This campaign was obviously less urgent. The confusions of that first Sunday, and succeeding Sundays, allowed people to stay away without being noticed. In the end, the Party was forced to send out its cadres to root out the parasites from their homes, and drive them out to work for the nation.

The last Sunday before I left, Party militants carried out a house-to-house search. They took care to make no distinction over age or health. Old women and little children, tired menfolk and nursing mothers all volunteered for work. They strutted from house to house, banging on doors and screaming at the people who answered them, pushing and hitting the citizens to urge on them a national spirit. They also took the opportunity to check out identity cards. By the time they reached us, we were dressed and ready to go. My father had insisted that we should not stir until they forced us out. I answered the door to three men. They looked very quickly behind me – *Get out. Get to work.* – and one of them pushed me aside and entered the house, shouting, it seemed, at the top of his voice. Without thinking I took hold of his grimy collar and pulled him back. When he was level with me, I helped him farther out with a shove on his chest.

The three moved together. They stepped back. Their manner changed from righteous resolution to caution. They were dirty and muscular, and looked like the people you would find anywhere where such work was required, sanguine bums who would mug old ladies to slake a psychosis of wounded dignity. One of them reminded me of the sleeveless man I had seen at Sood's. My father pushed me violently to one side.

'He's only a boy, only a boy!' he appealed to them.

I was hauled farther into the house, by my grandmother I think. The three men were angry, shouting at my father. He was mumbling his apologies and bobbing his head. I was called out to face the three men. The ragged man I had pulled out was now ready to release his anger in a few well-aimed blows. He detached himself from the rest and strode to within inches of me, emboldened by the indignant chorus of his companions. I felt very calm, and would have thrown myself on him without any further provocation had there been the need. Down the street our activities were drawing attention. The old man, dressed to go out, was watching with palpable fear. The evil-smelling cadre pointed an angry finger up my nostril.

'You'll get into trouble,' he shouted, spitting with anger. The other two added some obscenities and my father tried to interpose his body between the angry man and me. He was pushed angrily to one side. 'You listen to me,' said the man, still shaking and spitting with anger. 'You get out there and get to work or we'll deal with you. All of you, you scum. You think maybe you're master here?' All the three men grumbled at this liberty, bunching their fists and hissing through gritted teeth like melodramatic villains. I suppose they could have beaten me to death.

Up and down the street people had stopped to look and listen. I could see that this was making the three men nervous. Their fear was that they were about to be caught in a communal riot. There was no danger of that. We were too well-learned in the ways of submission, although this had not yet become fully clear to our tormentors.

'Show me your cards,' said the angry man. My father collected the cards and handed them over to the man. The three of them examined the dark photographs intently and then handed the cards back.

'Don't you want to check the names?' I asked them, letting them know that I knew they could not read.

'I'll kill you,' the man whispered angrily. He glanced round quickly at the crowd and swore. When they turned to go, insulting and abusing us as they went, they did not stop to knock on other houses down the street. The crowd cheered gleefully as they turned into the clearing. Some of the people started to go back to their houses. The old man shook his head and wagged a finger at me.

'That was stupid,' he said. 'Now we're all in trouble.' He smiled and winked at me. My father patted me on the back. I was a hero. 'You see what education does for these children. It makes them brave,' said the man.

We all volunteered that day. My father thought it would be wise not to ask for any more trouble. All was confusion as usual at the site. Nobody approached to give us any work. We waited until the sun was too strong and then went back home.

On the night before I left, my mother prepared a feast. The rug was taken out of its sacks, beaten and spread out in the guest-room. With the chairs pushed back against the wall, there was just enough space for all of us to squeeze in. As they had done throughout the long wait for the journey, they spoke of it as a mere formality. All talk of caution was dismissed. My father took all reference to it as an attempt at making a joke. In their company I found it easy to forget my own doubts. In that profusion of rich food and high optimism, it seemed that nothing was beyond me. The last clear-sighted words of advice were delivered, warnings and threats were unambiguously detailed, and the help of God was solemnly requested. Zakiya did not say anything all evening, but she smiled at me every time I looked at her.

I was to leave early in the morning. My father had insisted on accompanying me to the station, and refused to allow anyone else to come. *What's the fuss? I'll just walk with him on my way to work. You women always want to make a big thing out of nothing.* I went to bed that night filled only with thoughts of departure. It was only because my mother came back to me in the middle of the night to say goodbye again that I realised I had not spared a thought for her. We talked for a short while before she left me again, saying she had only come to wish me well for the last time and I was not to worry about anything.

I found it hard to sleep. I became frantic with the thought that if I did not sleep I would wake up in the morning feeling tired. Old doubts returned to mock the optimism of the evening. Old fears of the journey came back to keep me awake until the early hours.

Frightened by all the stories I had heard, I had insisted on travelling second rather than third class. That way I would be sure of a reserved bunk. Travelling third was a knees-up affair on ribbed wooden benches, by all accounts. My compartment was empty when I got on. I stowed away my suitcase under one of the bottom bunks as I had been advised. The compartment was panelled with wood. The upholstery was a green, soft plastic, cool to the touch. The tiny fountain under the window was operated by a long, tapering lever. The miniature basin cupped under the curved recd of the fountain, glinted like a new coin. There were curtains above the window, gathered at the corners and held back by straps. I pulled up the window and pushed my head out, as I had seen people do in the pictures. My father came down the platform to stand underneath me.

'What's it like?' he asked.

He had been amiable and pleasant, happy to talk. He reached up on tiptoe to try and see inside but he was not tall enough. I went out to the platform to say goodbye to him.

'Listen,' he said. 'I don't have much time. Be careful. Don't do anything stupid ... and come back to us. Do you understand? You must write and let me know. If there are any problems you write and let me know. Our hopes and good wishes go with you.'

He took my hand and squeezed it. I said *goodbye*, hoping he had finished. I wanted him to go before he embarrassed himself with absurd paternal emotions he did not feel. 'Be a good son, as you've always been,' he said, squeezing my hand again. His voice had become thicker, and I cringed as I saw him growing infatuated with his role. Suddenly he smiled, signalling that the performance no longer interested him. 'Don't come back with nothing,' he said in a more familiar voice. 'You do everything possible to persuade that thief to help you. We don't want anything for ourselves, just to do our duty by our son. This is not a holiday. Do you understand? Don't dishonour us, and don't come back with nothing.' He shook his head slightly as if he was not sure that I understood.

'Don't worry,' I said cheerfully.

He turned and walked back up the platform towards the barrier. As I watched him hurry away, I restrained an impulse to laugh. It seemed wrong. When I went back to the compartment, there was a man sitting on the bunk opposite mine. He was a young man, his head bent over a book. He looked up as I entered and greeted me with a smile and a nod. I sat down on my bunk, leaning out of the window, watching the activity on the platform. I was glad that my travelling companion was a young man. Soon the train began to hiss and blow in preparation for departure.

'Do you have the time?' The voice was very sure of itself. I turned to look at him and shake my head. I did not have a watch. He smiled, stood up and walked over to the window. His hair was cropped short, as if he was in the army or police. His face was lean and very black. He was built like an athlete. I glanced at the book he had left turned face down on the bunk: *Mine Boy* by Peter Abrahams.

'Why aren't we moving? It must be time now.' He looked at me as he said this, and looked for a moment longer than he needed to, as if studying me. He introduced himself as Moses Mwinyi, leaning forward to shake hands. 'How far are you going?' he asked, sitting down again and glancing casually at his book before shutting it and laying it beside him.

'Nairobi,' I said, trying to match his casual manner and his broad smile.

'So am I,' he said with an expanded grin. He waited a moment longer, grinning and nodding his head encouragingly. Something was expected of me. I grinned and nodded too. His smile waned a little. 'What are you called, man?' he asked finally, gently.

'I'm sorry,' I said, feeling stupid and discourteous. 'My name is Hassan. Hassan Omar.'

'Pleased to meet you, Hassan. Moses Mwinyi,' he said for the second time. He leaned back with a proud smile. I wondered whether I should know the name. He sighed and glanced out of the window again, becoming impatient with the train. 'Is this your home town?' he asked.

I nodded. He drew breath sharply and shook his head with commiseration. 'This place is dead,' he said with exaggerated finality. 'I've been here two days, and I don't mind telling you, brother, I've seen enough. There's nothing here but brothels and arse-fuckers. They should tear the place down and begin again. No offence, my friend.'

'Where are you from?' I asked.

'Dar es Salaam,' he said. 'The City of Dreams!'

From everything I had heard about that city, he was welcome to it. I was not anxious to demonstrate my ignorance by saying so, though. For then I would have to admit that I had never been there. 'I hear it's a very dusty and ugly town,' I said, unable to resist in the end. I was determined not to be intimidated by his confident smile and his athletic good looks.

'Ugly!' I could see he was not feigning the shock. 'We have supermarkets and five-star hotels and night-clubs. What have you got here? You should go and see for yourself.' The train hissed very loudly and jerked into action, lurching slowly past the platform. Moses glanced out of the window and grinned.

'I've got to put out a fire,' he said. 'I think I saw a toilet down the corridor. Will you keep any eye on my bag? There are a lot of hungry people on this train.'

I liked him. He seemed so unconcerned about things. Everything was new to me, the landscape, the train. I had lived there all my life and had never even thought twice about these things. In the near distance were clumps of bushes and trees which cut off the horizon. I was surprised at how quickly we were in the countryside.

This was only the second time I had been away from home. The first had been a school trip to Chwaka, ten whole days by the sea, to study tidal patterns or something. Ten delicious days of half-cooked fish and soggy pancakes! The teachers had insisted we cook for ourselves. At night we sat on the veranda of the beach-house and sang sentimental love songs. We sat on night-long vigils by the cemetery, waiting for the ghosts that never turned up. Hockey on the beach ... then somebody found a cave that smelt of leaf-mould and death. We found a cold pool in the depths of the cave, a shrine to an ancient water-god. We swam in it until the women came and threw stones at us for defiling their drinking water. It rained on the night before we left, and our thin mattresses were soaked and matted into gunny sacks. But what abandon in that run through the deluge past the cemetery to the sea! What delight to match the elemental rumpus with our own childish squeals and yells! Ten whole days by the sea.

The train swayed from side to side, hypnotic in its regularity, deafeningly noisy. A slight breeze blew in through the open window, ruffling the folds of the curtains held back by the straps. It looked hot outside.

We were expected to arrive in Nairobi the following morning. My mother had packed some food for me and

I knew I had a sheet for the night. I checked that my passport was still in my bag. I sat back, and put my feet up on the opposite bunk, relishing my new freedom. There was a knock on the door, followed immediately by the entrance of a short, plump old man. He stared at my feet, then pointed a fat finger at them.

'Off!'

He adjusted his cap, tugged at his tunic, squared his shoulders and asked for my ticket. There were no questions, no threats, no abuse. He patted his pockets and withdrew a pad. 'Bedding?' he asked. I shook my head. He wrote something down and put the pad away. 'First time to Nairobi?' he asked. I nodded. He looked slightly annoyed. I should have said something or smiled, but the words would not come. He yanked the door open and departed. I had not meant to be rude.

The seat was not as comfortable as it had at first seemed, clinging as it did to my moist back. I wanted to stretch my legs, have a look around but I did not want to leave Moses' bag unguarded. I didn't want to think about my uncle, not yet. When he intruded on my thoughts I pushed him back. Strangely, I was not at all afraid. Once the train was on the move I felt safe. The door opened again, slowly. Moses put his head round the door, then came in.

'He's gone,' he said. 'I don't have a ticket, you see.' He smiled at me, acknowledging my amazement. 'I never buy a ticket. These collectors are so dumb you don't need to. Twice a term I travel up and down, and not caught once. I'm a student at the University in Nairobi.'

He said this with his eyes lowered. I must have looked suitably impressed, for when he glanced up he smiled. 'Reading Literature,' he added, picking up his book and cradling it in interlocked hands. He put the book down beside him and glanced at me again. The glance gradually developed into a stare.

'Don't you say anything?' he asked, frowning. 'Are you all right?'

'Yes, yes,' I said, nonplussed by this direct assault.

'As I was saying, I never pay.'

'Yes, yes,' I said.

'You say this is your first time? Phew! You've got a lot to see. Nairobi's a great place. I really like it ... and the University's good. Except the food, of course. The mess they give us to eat is poison. Last year we went on strike. No more lectures until they fire the cook, or kill him. Yeah, we really went on strike.'

'Successful?' I asked, feeling a burden now to say something, to show interest.

'Not at first,' continued Moses, pleased with me. 'At first they brought in security guards, big Luos with heavy sticks. But the students just went berserk, chasing the guards all over the campus, breaking into buildings, smashing cars. It's true. So then they called in the army. I tell you, this Africa. We're savages. They killed one student and sent the rest of us home. When we came back, they fired the cook. Why couldn't they do that in the first place?'

'Is the food better now?'

He laughed. 'No, it's still poison.'

'Your studies ... what about them? Are they going well?'

He brushed my question aside, making a face. 'The city, that's what Nairobi's about. What a city!'

'Better than Dar es Salaam?'

'Eeh,' he chuckled. 'I only live in Dar, my people come from Kenya. Nairobi's the best in Africa, you'll see. Only you need to be a millionaire to enjoy it. And there are too many Indians.'

'Do you have to do a lot of reading for the course?' I asked, not wanting to hear another vengeful attack against Indians.

'You don't listen or what, eh? I'm telling you it's the night life that's the real life in Nairobi. You could start in the evening and you'd still be eating honey when morning comes. They have bodies in Nairobi that you won't find anywhere in East Africa ... black, white, Arab, Somali, Indian. The things they do ... '

He laughed, waiting for me to ask more questions. I must have looked disapproving. He looked suddenly serious and studious, picking his book up again. 'But don't think it's all fun,' he said admonishingly. 'You have to work very hard at the University. We're very lucky to be there. The future of our country's in our hands.'

The train was slowing down. Moses stuck his head out of the window, despite the warning not to do so. 'We're in the middle of nowhere,' he announced as he turned back in. 'Maybe the driver needs to go into the bushes. Shit, it's hot.'

He sat down and gingerly picked up a corner of his shirt with the tips of his fingers and flapped it, fanning himself. He picked up his book and fanned himself with it.

'Do you like Peter Abrahams?' I asked.

'Well, he's not a bad writer,' he said. 'He's too self-conscious, that's the problem. He doesn't write like an African. Do you know what this book reminds me of? Alan Paton. It has the same kind of liberal preaching, soft-nosed and confused. Do you know what I mean? There is no sense of identification with the mass of oppressed Africans.'

I went to look for the toilet as soon as the train was on the move again. It was late in the morning, and the sun was now brazen enough to distort distances and shapes. In the distance I could see the shadow of hills. The land was dry and empty. The wind was building up, whirling angry puffs of reddish dust across the plain. On the other side of the train I could see the escarpments of the central plateau, purplish and hazy.

I squeezed into the side of the carriage to allow two girls to pass. They giggled as they sidled past, pretty Indian girls, brushing their buttocks against my leg. Daddy was just behind them so I pretended not to notice.

Later the train stopped at a small dusty station. Nobody got off the train, and it was still too hot for anybody to think of stepping out for a stroll. An old lady sat on her own on the platform, leaning against the domed, whitewashed station building. It seemed an unnecessarily elaborate building for such a small pointless stop on the way to Nairobi. Perhaps the station was part of somebody's grandiose scheme which had not worked. Trussed-up live chickens were gathered round the old woman's feet, their heads moving with sudden, speculative movements, as if they knew what they were hoping to see but had not yet caught sight of it.

I wanted to eat my food and wondered if Moses had any of his own. He seemed pleased by the offer that he should share mine. I spread out the bread and the chicken that my mother had packed for me.

We stopped at the station for about a quarter of an hour. As the train built up steam, preparing to pull out, the old lady gathered her wares, holding the chickens upside down by their trussed legs. No official of the railways had appeared in all the time we had been there. None appeared as we were leaving. Nobody had got off, and I had not seen anybody get on. It was a mysterious stop in the middle of nowhere, at a mysteriously elaborate station without a name-board. Moses looked puzzled when I mentioned it, then suggested that perhaps the train had stopped to rest.

Moses went away and came back a few minutes later with a bag of plums. He would not say where he had got them from. I suspect he stole them. He put the bag between us, among the remains of the chicken. He was talking and laughing about everything, enjoying himself. We drank water from the miniature fountain, bending down to suck at the spout.

'This thing reminds me of my little brother pissing,' he said. 'Trickle, trickle.'

We reached the arid plateau in the early evening. There was not much to see. I was glad that I was just passing through this hostile land, and not part of it. We drew the curtains early and stretched out on the bunks. It turned out that Moses had no bedding of any kind, so I lent him a *kikoi*.

'I like travelling light,' he said, drawing the *kikoi* round him. 'And I'm creating the opportunity for a kind fellow traveller to do a good deed. I'm hungry again.'

We went to bed without supper. I insisted that we should keep what was left of the bread for breakfast. I had not reckoned on sharing my food, although I did not mind doing so. I was glad of Moses' company.

'So what do you do with yourself when you're not playing an explorer?' he asked as we lay in the gentle swaying of the speeding train.

'Nothing. I've just finished school.'

He grunted in the dark. 'I know the time. Looking for prospects, hoping that somebody will smile kindly on you. I was lucky. I was the best student in my school so it was easy for me. I went straight to university. You know in my school I was the head prefect. Azania High School. I mean, that's something.' He sat up, leaning on one elbow and was silent for a while, contemplating his own greatness.

'So it was easy for me. I'm doing Literature. I can take it or leave it, you know, this Literature. I did well in it at school, and I knew my teacher wanted me to do it. The headmaster thought it was a good idea too. Literature is life, he used to say. The stupid old shit. What did he know about life?'

'Why did you do it then? Why didn't you do what you wanted?'

'All I wanted was a degree. I wanted a car, a fine house, chicken for dinner and some fancy women. I thought Literature would be easy.' He peered at me, waiting. I nodded for him to continue. 'And it is easy. It's shit. All this humanities stuff is shit. All we have is African Art, African Literature, African History, African Culture and all that shit. And we can't even make a screwdriver or a tin of talcum powder for ourselves. It's technology we need. Now everything we use we have to get from Europe or America. They even give us money to buy these things. We have to learn to build our own factories, make our own motor cars, weave our own cotton ... That's the secret. Until then, all this stuff is shit.'

He was leaning forward, straining to emphasise his words. 'Listen,' he continued. 'Maybe in order to grow we'll just have to forget about African Art for a while.' He smiled and shifted position. 'I'm even prepared to forget about African people for a while. What's the point of spending millions to build hospitals for some of these primitive tribals? When they get better you have to spend more millions to feed them. They don't produce anything or do anything. I would shoot them. If it takes the murder of a few thousand savages to make ourselves strong, then so be it. It will be worth it for our children.' He paused to see if I would object.

When I did not, he leaned farther forward, anxious to persuade. I guessed that this was a favourite thesis. 'This talk of tradition and African this and African that is just more African Art. These people take us for fools. They don't mean it, these champions of tradition. The only tradition they're interested in is making their buttocks fat. What we need is a strong man with a vision, a Stalin. Instead we have these greasy chiefs who are only interested in dirty money and other people's women. They talk about the dignity of the black man and then kick him in the teeth. They take us for fools.' He sat up, his feet touching the floor. 'They play on our greed, you see.'

'Where will your sacrifices begin?' I asked.

'No, don't joke. These people just don't think. Look at the way they're treating these Indians. It's stupid. So what if they came here and made a lot of money? So what if they refused to become citizens? They have expertise. They have money. Let's make use of them first, then we can throw the bastards out. We don't throw the white man out. We're too afraid of him. We want him to like us. African Art, African History ... we plead with them to think of us as human beings. But the Indian we persecute and chase out. We're behaving like children. It's demoralising.'

'I said where will your sacrifices begin? Which *tribals* will you start with? When will it be the turn of the Indians? When will you move on to the Arabs, or the Somalis? And who will be your next scapegoat after that?'

'Scapegoats! That's the problem,' he thundered. 'That's why we don't do anything. We all see ourselves as victims, waiting our turn. Waiting for somebody to come from out there and give us a helping hand. We don't do anything for ourselves. Who'll be next? Well, we'll be next ... sooner or later. Unless we do something about it.'

'Do what? Make sacrifices ... of other people?'

He made me nervous. I had heard people say the same things before. I may even have said them myself, but never with such passion and conviction. We said many foolish things that were part of our frustration as we witnessed the plundering of our nations. Moses spoke as if he believed in what he was saying, but I doubted that he was doing more than we were.

'We are victims,' I said. 'And maybe you're right, that we sit and wait and do nothing. What would you have people do in the face of such violence? Sacrifices are made every day. Somebody or other is plucked out and sacrificed for the advancement of our nation. It provides all of us with a powerful hint of the might of our state. And we can all run around like frightened mice, whispering about conspiracies and slaughters. It's a sport our masters provide for us.'

'Sport!' he said angrily. 'What do you think we are? Savages? You're making us sound like bloodthirsty natives out of a Tarzan movie.'

'You're the one who doesn't mind killing tribals and Indians.'

'If necessary,' he shouted. 'If we have to kill those who are holding us back or exploiting us, then I say let's do it.'

I watched him leaning forward and huffing with the passion of his defence, and I realised that I was enjoying provoking him. 'Shall we do it before or after you get your degree and your house and car?' I asked him.

'That's unfair,' he said, leaning back.

'This is just high-sounding hate, Moses. You talk of killing as if it is a game. What kind of price is that to pay for progress?'

'No price is too much,' he said, waving a finger at me. 'Until we do things for ourselves, and don't have to go begging from these white people every day of the week, you can forget progress or justice or any of that business. And if it's only a Stalin who can do that, then I say let's have him.'

We had got nowhere, but he was watching me with a smile, secure in the invincibility of his argument. 'I hope Stalin will still let you go whoring in night-clubs,' I said.

He laughed, prepared to be generous now that he felt I had conceded to him. I lay down on my bunk. He switched the light off, still chuckling in the darkness as he settled himself down. I wondered what he would be doing in a few years' time, whether he would have learnt the cynicism that would make the memory of such passion seem an absurd illusion. I heard him shuffling, reaching into his bag, and then turning the water on.

'What are you doing?' I asked. 'Pissing in the basin?'

He laughed. 'No, just going to squeeze some juices out. Do you want the soap?'

'You're masturbating,' I said, part admiring, part amused.

'Yeah, yeah,' he said, sighing and blowing, while his hand beat a lather out of the soap. 'You're throwing me off my stride, man. You want the soap or not?'

'No,' I said. 'I don't want the soap.'

I pulled the sheet over my head and closed my mind to the noise. I think I fell asleep at once. I woke up feeling cold, and instantly remembered with pleasure where I was. The sun was pouring in through the thin curtains but it was not yet warm enough to dispel the chill. Moses was still asleep, lying on his back. He looked vulnerable with his mouth half-open and with one arm cramped to his side. I dressed quietly so as not to disturb him. I knew we would be arriving in a few hours and I wanted to be ready. He had seen all this before but to me it was all new, and I did not want to miss anything. The corridor was still deserted, and

I toyed with the thought that Moses and I were the only passengers on the train.

The toilet was occupied. I stood by the door to wait, but the gut-curdling eruptions on the other side of the door drove me farther away. I wondered whether I should go away and come back later, but the pressure on my bladder demanded more immediate attention. And what could the poor man emptying his gut in the closet do that was worse than the crusted squalor of the latrine holes at home?

The land we were travelling through seemed dark and fertile, on the verge of being lush. The hills were endlessly rolling towards the purple horizon. The train lurched heedlessly on, its indifference almost joyous and carefree, like a preoccupied runner waving to passers-by but intent on the happiness that lay ahead. The green hillsides were hunched contentedly, fecund and swollen with complacency. They were in every way unlike the overbearing oppression of the narrow streets of our town, with its aromas of past cruelties and entangled jealousies. It was no wonder that people had learnt to fight for this land, to murder and maim for it. Who would think to risk so much for a squalid, slippery alleyway?

Near at hand, the verges of the railway tracks were choked with tall grass that even in the limp chill of the morning light looked venomous and sharp.

The door of the toilet opened and a tall man staggered out. He seemed to have difficulty steadying himself. After his exertions, it was a wonder that he could walk at all. I waited until he had staggered away, then reluctantly approached the toilet. I took a deep breath, threw the door open and hurled myself in before my resolve weakened.

A man was lying on the floor, wedged between the pedestal and the partition wall, his knees pulled up and spread

89

apart. I moved back and shut the door. It was nothing to do with me. I went in again. He seemed to be asleep. His breathing was laboured and heavy. His shirt was spattered with blood, but there was no sign of a wound. His arms were jammed by his side, as if they had been forced into the narrow space. His face was swollen and puffed with bruises. Gently, I kicked his foot. He groaned once, and then opened and closed his mouth without making another sound. It was nothing to do with me. I moved back and closed the door behind me.

I heard voices coming down the corridor. The tall man was coming back, followed by the ticket-collector. The official was shouting, pushing the tall, thin man ahead of him. When they reached the door, the tall man pushed me roughly to one side, and I saw that one side of his face was glossy with blood. He pointed at the door, waiting for the official to go in ahead of him. The ticket-collector had not had time to button up his tunic and chose to do this now. He had difficulty with the top button, but eventually he clipped that round the heavy folds of his neck.

'You!' he said, turning to me, and practising on me the splendour of his authority. 'Are you anything to do with this? I'll have you and the rest of them thrown out at the next station. Where do you think you are?'

'I was just waiting to go in there,' I protested, hearing and hating the frightened whine in my voice. 'It's nothing to do with me.'

'Get out of here, then,' said the tall man.

'You shut up,' said the official, wagging a warning finger at him. 'That booze is still going round in your head, is it? Nobody asked you to give any orders. You'd better mind yourself, or I'll have you locked up at the next station.' He waited until the tall man had dropped his eyes in defeat before he turned to me. 'You! Isn't it enough to have grown men drinking themselves to sickness without having people hanging about, staring as if they have nothing better to do? Come on, get out of here.'

The noise had woken some people up, and as the faces made their dishevelled appearance from behind doors, the official turned to them for sympathy. I squeezed past him, and then past the tall man. He turned the injured side of his face away from me.

'What's going on up there?' a man asked me as I made my way back.

'I think somebody is hurt,' I said.

He looked quickly up the corridor and then back at me, as if to make sure that I was not playing a cruel joke on him. He hurried away to see for himself. I found Moses still asleep. The ease of his slumber irritated me. It seemed callous and insensitive in the circumstances. I was tempted to shake him awake, but the thought of the demands his conversation would make dissuaded me. I would probably only get a robust and knowing summary of my naïvety. I shifted my eyes from him and tried to think of what lay ahead.

I had enough bread left for breakfast, although I would probably have to share it. I would have to take a taxi to my uncle's house when we arrived. My father had written to him to tell him the date of my arrival, but I expected that he would be too busy or would forget. I knew very little about him. I had never met him, but in the months before my journey many of the stories I had heard as a child about him had been revived. I knew that he had made a lot of money selling cars, and that he had worked himself into a position of respect. My father said that he had made big money out of smuggling. I had no idea how true that was.

I did not know how rich he was, and whether he could afford to lend or give me the money to study. My mother had told me as much as she could, so she said. I sensed that she was holding things back, and that what she told me was more the legend than the reality. She had spoken of his vile temper, his bear-like rages. I told her that I had had a lot of practice at those and would do my best not to provoke them. At other times she described him as generous to a fault. Yes, I could see that in the way that he had done nothing for his sister while she lived in poverty a few hundred miles away. I suspected that I was on a futile quest. Yet, he had invited me to go. Perhaps ... No, it was silly to assume that a brother who would do nothing for his poverty-stricken sister – and good luck to him if that was how he wanted to live – would willingly part with thousands for her son.

Still, there was nothing to be lost but a little dignity. The worst that could occur would be to seem foolish. And here was the opportunity to travel and see the world, to breathe in a different air and sense freedom nuzzling the leash. Cross the swamps and sail down the Nile, all the way to Alexandria. Perhaps my arrival would shame the rich uncle into an orgy of generosity, reparation for his previous neglect. He will not fail to be impressed by my sagacity and my integrity, and at the very least will burn with bitter shame for his refusal to help such a paragon in his selfless search for even greater wisdom. For the moment it was enough to be on the move, to be in the running, to have escaped the suffocation of those narrow alleyways.

I went in search of another toilet. There were people in the corridors now, and the train was more crowded than when we started out. The compartment was empty when

I returned, and I ate what was left of my bread before Moses came back. He returned wearing my *kikoi*, cleaning his teeth with a plastic brush. He bent over the basin for a few moments, spitting and scrubbing and washing his mouth out. He dried himself with a corner of my *kikoi*. He looked completely refreshed, happy to be alive. He rubbed his palms up and down his cheeks and smiled. I envied him. My smile felt pale and sickly compared to his.

'Somebody's hurt,' he said, ripping the *kikoi* off without any inhibitions. 'Some fucking drunk. Somebody beat him up good and stole his money. He was covered in blood. I tell you, there are some mean bastards around. I remember once in Nairobi ... '

He paused and I assumed he was marshalling his story together. He zipped up his trousers, stood undecided, then smiled and shook his head. 'Too early for that sort of thing,' he said. 'We get something to eat first.'

'I've eaten,' I said, feeling ashamed.

I don't think he believed me. He must have assumed I was too broke to afford breakfast. 'On me,' he said. 'You know, we must arrange to meet in Nairobi. You must come and see me at the University. Just ask for Moses Mwinyi. We'll go out some place, do some whoring. And I'll show you some of my poems. Oh yes, does that surprise you?' He stood by the door waiting for me.

'No,' I said. 'I really don't want anything.'

He shrugged, closed the door behind him and left me to pick up my *kikoi* off the floor. I examined it for marks of his previous night's abuse but it seemed clean. There was little else to do but sit by the window and gaze at the hills. The tall brown grass was quivering gently in the wind, little waves of motion on the silent hills, silent now with a primeval patience. In the distance were scattered bushes of whistling thorn. The train had lost its joyous step, moving slowly, gruntingly on the final haul.

As we approached Nairobi, the Ngong hills were visible in the west. Moses pointed them out to me, and we laughed with pleasure at the sight of them. A plane, coming in to land, passed over our heads, throwing us into a flurry of dashes from one window to another.

'It's good to be back,' Moses said, leaping back into the compartment. 'You really must come and see me.'

He picked up his bag, explained that he would have to look sharp if he was to avoid being caught by the railway officials, and shook hands. I was sorry to see him go. He reminded me again that I must visit him at the University, smiled pleadingly and waved farewell.

4

The station was large. Did it need to be that grand? Unexpectedly, I did not panic. I showed my ticket and was allowed to go through without a single question. It was hot and I felt stale and greasy with sweat. I clung to my travel-stained musk for comfort. I remember the press of people, the shouting, the many varieties of uniform. It was what more romantic travellers would have described as the zest for life that was unmistakably African, the dance that was part of the natural rhythm of life. I found the crowd confusing and frightening. I kept my eyes to the ground, jostling the crowd but unable to resist its momentum. I kept a tight grip on my bag, expecting a hand to grab for it and wrestle it from me.

The crowd deposited me outside. I was too confused to see very much of the city as the taxi drove me through it. I remember being pleased that the wide roads and the tall stone buildings were as impressive as I had hoped. They suggested both wealth and order. The pavements were crowded with people. I tried to be calm, tried hard not to give the impression that I was a country boy who had just arrived in town. Our seaside town had been in existence for three centuries before Nairobi had even been thought of, I reminded myself. We were trading with China before the railways that gave birth to this conceited works-depot had even been invented. What was there to fear? The taxi-driver was silent and sullen, interested neither in the crowd nor in his passenger. He handled the car with grim determination, only once muttering angrily when an Indian boy leapt off the pavement and ran across the road in front of us.

We seemed to drive for a long time before we reached the rich residential district where my uncle lived. I saw the growing magnificence of the houses with relief. Rumours transform a poor man's good fortune to such an extent that his modest breeze-block bungalow becomes a palace. These things happen. It was a relief to find that thus far the legend round my uncle was true. *Salaam aleikum, ami Ahmed. Ahlan wa sahlan, ya nurullah. Good morning, sir*, I practised.

The house we stopped at did not have a hedge, unlike most of the others we had passed. Instead there was a wrought-iron chain separating the front garden from the road. Most of the front garden was lawn. There were bushes closer to the house, and a large blooming hibiscus by the door. By the side of the house was a mature flame-tree, with some stunted ornamental palms behind it. The taxi-driver hooted, waved and drove off. A little surprised by this sudden bonhomie, I was too slow in waving back and the car had disappeared behind next door's hedge before I had raised my arm to respond.

I hoped that by now I had been observed from the house. In the face of such gentility my errand seemed stupid and vulgar. The door was locked, but I was ready for this. I put my bag down and straightened myself for my first doorbell. I expected it to ring gently, echoing down corridors, so the harsh jangle on the other side of the door surprised me and almost destroyed my composure. I thought I had done it wrong. I waited, worrying whether I should ring it again.

A girl opened the door. She leant against it, enquiring my purpose with raised eyebrows and an impatient thrust of the chin. 'Yes?'

I remember the sense of grievance and hurt I felt at this treatment. *I'm not a beggar*, I thought as I scowled at her. She moved off the door and leant back a bit, as if to get a better look at me. *Any moment now she's going to call for help*. She examined me, running her eyes quickly over my clothes and my bag.

'My name is Hassan Omar,' I started on a speech I had prepared for the occasion. Her eyes twinkled. I realised I had spoken in English. She folded her bare arms across her chest, shifted her weight on to one leg and sighed.

'Yes?' she repeated. She was now preparing to enjoy this little event. I could not help smiling. She smiled back, a mere twitching of the lips, ironic and unamused. She pushed her chin forward again aggressively, peremptorily. I smiled again, unprepared for this petulance.

'I'm calling on Bwana Ahmed bin Khalifa,' I said, speaking more correctly and deliberately.

'He's not in,' she said. She unfolded her arms and reached for the door, bracing her legs for the grand slam.

'I've come to see him,' I said quickly.

'Well, he's not here,' she said less abruptly.

'He knows I'm coming,' I said, bending down to pick up my bag. I was tempted by the idea of turning on my heel and striding angrily away. That would make plain my wounded dignity, and would make her sorry.

'Yes?' she said, waiting for an explanation. I took comfort from her tone of voice, and from the watchful, searching way she looked at me.

'He's expecting me,' I said, sensing an ascendancy, and vaguely regretting that I was not to be turned away after all. I made a movement towards the door and she hesitated for a moment before stepping aside to let me in. I wiped my feet carefully and at length on the doormat. I had heard stories of friends walking shit and mud off the streets into such houses. I bent down to take off my plimsolls, and I sensed her agitation behind me. Her hand touched me on my shoulder, merely a flutter, without pressure.

'You don't have to take your shoes off,' she said.

I straightened, feeling foolish. She smiled, reassuringly. She was now feeling sorry for me. So I shrugged, to show that I was not bothered by such things. We all make mistakes. I did not think to protest at the time that where I came from to wear shoes inside a house was impolite. She must have thought I was just being embarrassingly obsequious.

'Welcome,' she said, motioning me down the hallway and leading off ahead of me. Gentle colours covered the walls and the floor. The deep lilac looked yielding and thick like a rug. The carpet was a very delicate, silky brown. A brass chest stood in a corner of the hallway, under the netted window, and on it stood a tall fluted vase containing bougainvillaea bloom. I could sense my shoulders hunching forward deferentially in the presence of this wealth.

She led me into a large room, filled with light. One wall was almost all glass, and through it I could see the garden. Didn't the boys in the neighbourhood throw stones in Nairobi? This was the kind of house that Moses wanted to kill all those tribals for, I thought. The garden stretched away on a slope, tilting gently towards the fence at the bottom. I could see trees and passion-fruit bushes at the bottom of the garden. She pointed to a chair by the fireplace, a huge chair upholstered in the same maroon as the carpet. I put my bag down beside it and turned to thank her. She had gone. I peered at the fireplace, which was clean and swept out, and looked as if it had never been used. I tried to imagine a little boy going up the narrow hole to sweep the chimney, and imagination failed. I sank into the chair, so far that I gasped with surprise. *Country boy comes to town.*

The radio was playing so softly that it required a search to find it tucked away on the other side of the fireplace. There was a sudden scream from the garden, and I rushed to the open glass doors to see what it was. A large grey bird had just taken to the air, its wings beating lazily before it sank behind the slope of the hill. I wondered if they had pet peacocks as well. Somebody laughed loudly, and I craned my neck to try and trace the source. I went back to the chair, but kept an eye on the garden door.

She returned through an archway on the right. Evidently it was through there that she had disappeared in the first place. She was carrying a small silver tray on which stood a large jug and two glasses. She put the tray on the table nearest to me and then knelt down beside it. I was made uncomfortable by the intimacy. She smiled as she handed me my glass.

'Welcome,' she said. 'I know who you are now. I remembered while I was in the kitchen. You're my cousin, aren't you? You should have told me that. Daddy told me you would be coming, but I didn't remember the date. How was the journey?'

Daddy! She had used the English word. I knew it. And I felt sure that they would eat with knives and forks and have afternoon tea. 'I had a very good journey, thank you. This is very nice juice. What is it?'

'Passion-fruit,' she said. Scattered on her face were tiny little spots that had swelled into pimples on her forehead. I did not find them at all unattractive. She smiled again, and then rose with her glass in her hand. 'You must be very tired,' she said. 'I'll see if there's a room ready ... and

99

perhaps you'd like to have a wash and rest. Would you like something to eat?'

She excused herself and departed under the archway. I saw her a few moments later striding across the garden. I was her slave. As if seeing Nairobi was not enough, to find oneself under the same roof as such a lovely girl ... I would only worship from a distance of course, feast over her smell when she came too near, hope to coax a smile from her now and then.

A man entered the room through the archway and I rose to greet him. He was too young to be my uncle, perhaps about thirty or so. He was very thin, his eyes popping out of his face, his arms dangling by his side. My first thought was that he was a relation.

'Ahlan,' I said in greeting.

'Good morning, sir,' he said in English.

He lowered his head, hunched his shoulders and clasped his hands together. He came forward with his head lowered and tilted a little to one side. He bent down and picked up my bag. I reached out to retrieve it and he moved a step back, hand raised palm upward. I guessed that this performance was ironic.

'Mr Hassan, let me show you your room, sir,' he said. He sounded a little offended, sharp, but in his eyes, I thought I saw suppressed laughter. *And fuck you too.* He indicated another door, across the room from the archway. He strolled on ahead of me, did not bother to look back to see if I was following. They were all so mighty with poor country boy. I wondered what had been said about me before my arrival. It was hard to believe that this thin, well-dressed man was a servant. Servants wore rags during working hours. He led me down a short corridor, with rooms going off on either side. He stopped at the last door on the left, opened it and motioned me into the room ahead of him.

The room was large and airy. The sun was pouring in through the window. The white walls and white furniture made the room look brighter, cleaner. I was overwhelmed by the idea of such comfort, such privacy. What I had seen of the rest of the house should have prepared me, but I had never dreamed of sleeping in such a room. The bed was tucked away in the corner, and a large wardrobe stood at the foot of it. Opposite the bed was a desk and chair. A reading lamp on a stand leant over the easy chair under the window.

'Thank you,' I said.

'It's the best guest-room. I hope you like it,' he said. 'If you want to have a wash, I'll unpack for you.'

He was still carrying my bag, and with those words he raised it a little and glanced at it. 'No, no,' I protested. He seemed to wince. 'I haven't got much to unpack,' I explained. He waited for more, not yet mollified, not yet feeling that he had drawn enough blood.

'It's only a small bag,' I said.

'Yes, sir,' he said, putting my bag down.

'Thank you very much,' I said, indicating the room.

He bowed! He *bowed*. 'The bathroom is next door,' he said softly, standing at the door. 'My name is Ali.' *And I am Genghis Khan. How are you?* I guessed that Ali was the servile sobriquet, his professional title. 'If there is anything you require just ask me for it. I hope you enjoy your stay with us, Mr Hassan.'

He closed the door softly behind him, and no doubt his face broke into a smug grin as soon as the door was between us. I bowed at the closed door and tried to think of an obscene gesture but my heart was not in it. I would probably have done the same. I took out a clean shirt and put my bag away in the wardrobe. There was no point unpacking just to give bleary-eyes a good laugh. I laid the shirt on the bed and went off in search of the bathroom.

It fulfilled all expectations. I took off my plimsolls and walked barefoot on the blue tiles. I inhaled the perfume of the toilet disinfectant and tested the small extractor fan above the window. While I ran the bath, I ransacked the contents of the mirrored cabinets. I felt certain I could hear soft music in the air.

Bwana Ahmed bin Khalifa came home for lunch.

I was lying on the bed, luxuriating in my pampered solitude, and feeling remorse that I had deprived Ali of his name, when a knock on the door informed me of the master's arrival. I put on my clean shirt, tried a couple of smiles on the mirror, selected the more humble and went off in search of a future.

Ali led me into the living-room, then ushered me into the garden, standing aside to let me pass. I went out through the open glass doors on to the oval-shaped terrace. As I walked down the steps to the lawn, a cool breeze raced towards me, sniffed at me and raced past. The trees and bushes shuddered for a moment, and then were still. I could see a short, well-built man standing under one of the trees, talking to the girl. The sweat was running down my back and my arms were trembling a little. I felt I was about to make a fool of myself, but there was no helping it now. They were too engrossed in their affairs to notice my approach. I stopped a few feet away, and after a moment, I turned to admire the garden. I was obviously to be kept waiting. Lines of chalk were drawn on the lawn, faded by the sun and rain but still clear. The thorny bougainvillaea was garishly in flower, bright reds and purple mingling with rustic yellow and faded pink. Under the terrace were large hibiscus bushes, their waxy blooms leaning leeringly towards the ground. Jasmine and rose bushes filled the borders to the hedge. The bougainvillaea ran all the way down one side of the garden, viciously twisting on itself to form an impenetrable barrier. The passion-fruit bushes at the bottom of the garden were trained along the wires of the fence. Heavy, yellow fruit was hanging off the branches, some spotted by the beaks of feeding birds. I felt ridiculous standing there in the sun while the sweat ran off me.

I sensed them turning to look at me, and heard a sharp intake of breath. *What! Is it you? I didn't see you standing there, dear fellow* ... I suppose that is what it was meant to suggest. I walked over towards them, right hand extended, a glad smile on my face and in my eyes. No glum looks from me! I was out to charm. Bwana Ahmed bin Khalifa came forward to meet me, walking with short measured steps, deliberately taking his time. There was an amused smile on his face. I assumed it was the one he reserved for poor nephews. His hair was flecked with grey, and his trimmed moustache bristled with steely lines of white metal. I pounced on him with my wide-open hand, caressed his reverently, gulping for air in my excitement, and then returned the limp appendage to him. To my horror I found that I was enjoying this self-abasement. I could not feel my face smiling. Perhaps the muscles had returned to their usual glum repose. I swung my lips wider apart, and threw in a powerful chuckle for good measure. They both laughed heartily, assuming that I was clowning.

'So,' said my uncle Ahmed bin Khalifa. His sister would have been proud to see how he had turned out, would have quailed at his musk of power and charisma. I remembered

Moses and his prayers for a Stalin. 'You made it all right then. Did you have a good journey?'

Did I detect a hint of disappointment in his voice? Was he hoping the lions of Voi would savage me? Did he think the white-slavers would get me and flog me off to the porn shops of Amsterdam? He was holding the hand I had shaken a little away from his body, as if he were being careful not to soil his clothes. He saw me glance at it, and he plunged the hand into his trouser pocket. He unbuttoned his jacket and gently stroked the crease of his trousers. He stroked for a moment his thin well-groomed moustache. His eyes were still amused, with just a shade of irritation in them. His face still smiled – I see that smile now, assured, patient. He turned to the girl and exchanged a quick flash of eyebrows with her. She smiled openly, looking curiously at the two of us. Did they think I was blind?

'Well, we'd better get out of this sun. Shall we go and see what the chef has got for our lunch?' he asked. 'How's your mother? Is she well?'

He led off ahead of us, talking in careful, correct tones over his shoulder. This was not a man to be taken in with greasy smiles. He did not seem the kind of man to be taken in at all. He was forbidding, and I imagined him to have a whole list of things that were not allowed in his presence, and a whole range of manners and courtesies whose function was only to swell his own dignity. I had walked into a lion's den, into the cyclops' cave. Where was the fierce temper? I was going to do my best not to find out. Who could imagine this calm, self-assured money-bags bursting forth with invectives and obscenities like my dear father. This was not one to weaken with tales of an idealistic love of knowledge. *Nothing gave me greater pleasure than to curl up under the glow*

and then hurling the empty air at his face. I nodded to show that I had understood. Food was ready and could I go and wash. Was he drunk? He waved goodbye, articulating his wrist the way a little child would. He showered me with large smiles and then left, shutting the door gently. I hurried to the bathroom. Having slept so long in the afternoon, I knew I would find it impossible to sleep at night. I must have been more tired than I realised.

I changed into a clean shirt for the third time in a day. I would have to do some washing before I went to bed. The plimsolls were nowhere to be seen. I found them outside the door, cleaned and coddled, the side-flap mended, the canvas brilliant and stiff, the hole in the toe-cap gaping black and jagged like a nasty wound.

They were waiting in the living-room, sunk in the deep, crimson chairs. The radio was playing softly. My uncle rose to greet me, smiling and ushering me into a chair. He had changed into a baggy, white, short-sleeved shirt, its pockets bulging with tobacco pouch and pipe.

'Did you have a good rest?' he asked, laughing at me. 'Not used to travelling, eh? It's more tiring than you think, isn't it?'

He sat opposite me, smiling and being friendly. This was how I had imagined him in my better moments, down to the baggy shirt, bulging pipe and tobacco, the very picture of the prosperous merchant genially at play. The radio was next to his head, and he leaned over and switched it off. The girl stirred at that and looked quickly away before her irritation showed. He saw it, though, and smiled at her averted face. She had changed again, and was now wearing a loose cream-coloured blouse. It had a dull, expensive-looking sheen and I wondered if it was silk. She looked beautiful, composed and in control. There was unmistakable pride in the way her father glanced at her. She looked at my shoes and smiled.

'Chinese,' I said, thinking to excuse their dilapidation with this explanation.

'Aaah,' she said. Her neck was taut with effort as she stretched forward to take a close look at my shoes. I caught a glimpse of the mound of her breasts, and quickly dropped my eyes. 'A work of art,' she said, mocking my nervousness.

The father, too, leant forward with a look of serious attention. 'Does the hole come with the shoe or did you have it put in specially?'

I joined them in their smiles, taking this teasing as a kind of welcome. I tried to think of something clever and self-deprecating to say, but all I felt was a resentment that I was forced to talk about shoes at all. 'They're in a terrible state, aren't they? They were good value, though.'

'Do you have a lot of Chinese things at home now?' he asked. 'The only Chinese things I've seen here are of very poor quality.'

'They're cheap,' I said.

'Buy cheap, pay later,' said my uncle, grinning at his own wit.

'Whatever you pay for shoes like that, I can't imagine that they are worth it,' said the girl. 'You should give them to somebody.'

She did not smile as she said this, but looked away a moment later with just a hint of shame in her averted face. Ali appeared to call us to dinner, and to let my poor shoes out of purgatory. The food was already on the table. Ali hovered at the kitchen door, with the idiot grin on his face. Uncle Ahmed winked at me to show me that he knew that the servant was behaving in a strange way.

'What do we have today, Ali?' he asked. 'I hope you remembered that we have a guest. What have you prepared for us?'

I could have told him that. I had been smelling it from the moment I opened my eyes, and my nose registered the unmistakable aromas of a biriani. Ali did not reply, but lined the plates in front of the large earthenware pot. When we were all seated, he lifted the lid and grinned triumphantly at all of us.

'It *is* biriani,' yelled the girl, clapping her hands with delight.

I struggled not to drown in the rivers of saliva that were pouring into my mouth. Who was the pantomime for? They must have known it was biriani. Who could mistake the aromas of that noble dish? Ali heaped spoonful after spoonful on the plates. The yellow grains glistened on the plates like pieces of quartz. Large lumps of meat squatted among the rice, dripping juices and fat. He served me last, at my insistence, and I let him pile up the plate until I felt that to ask for any more would be to advance from the childish clown to a greedy boor. He showed me his gums with a cook's delight. My hand slipped and slid among the meat and the rice. I took a mouthful and chewed slowly, surrendering to the sweetness of the marrow-soft meat. Ali was watching with open-mouthed pleasure. I sighed with contentment and they all laughed. Ali gave me another piece of meat as my reward. *This is more like it*, I commended myself. *The poor relation who is too much of a clown to realise what a cunt he's making of himself. Country boy comes to town and drools like a rehabilitated rag-picker over every mouthful of decent food.*

'You like it?' Ali asked with patronising glee. He spent the meal by my side, asking me questions about my progress,

109

adding a little historical information about the development of the meal, from its constituent lumps to the creation that was undermining the very fibres of my provincial self-identity. I warned myself not to overdo it, or else they would think I was laughing at them. Every now and again Ali would discover a morsel buried under the tumbling grains, and with a cry of delight he would drag it out and lay it on my plate. Was I being fattened for … ? Every time I paused he became anxious, waiting for me to resume. He dominated the conversation with anecdotes about food. I was surprised that my uncle let him carry on so, and I began to wonder if he was part of a complicated private joke that I did not understand. Ali was a different man from the supercilious servant who had served us lunch. Perhaps this was his real self, I thought. Perhaps the disdainful man I had seen earlier was more a victim of gloomy thoughts and tragic prognostications than a man at his best. There was something out of control about the way he was jigging beside me. Bwana Ahmed showed no impatience, indeed he smiled, interested and amused by Ali's performance.

I heard him address his daughter as Salma. Salma with the beautiful grey eyes! It was, naturally, important that her name had not been given to me. I was not to see her as somebody I could address willy-nilly as the mood took me. She said little, content to follow the conversation with her eyes. The attention she paid to my clowning was amused, but she was distant and preoccupied, as if dissociating herself. A stray smile appeared now and then, the way it does when one is watching a tiresome child playing. When my gluttony was sated I leant back in my chair, ashamed of my evening's work.

'Now I know what it's like to be rich,' I said, grinning at my host.

It was the wrong thing to say, graceless and carrying a hint of blame. Bwana Ahmed smiled unhappily, accepting the attention I had drawn to my poverty. Salma looked at me as if she had just noticed me. *That made you sit up, didn't it, poppet? Smelling the revolution in the air.* Ali moved away from me at last, and I realised how tense his presence by my shoulder had made me. I glanced again at Salma and found to my surprise that she was still looking at me. I looked guiltily at Bwana Ahmed. He was staring at her. She wiped the smile off her face the moment her eyes made contact with his. She returned his gaze, and I saw her thrust her chin forward the way she had done with me earlier. I watched the little drama with anxiety. I did not want my uncle to start becoming suspicious of me. Surely there was no cause! Surely my charm and stunning looks had not wounded her heart already! I wanted him to think me a harmless, ridiculous young man, an idiot worthy of his generosity. Surely no cause for alarm! The girl turned to me again, sitting straight in her chair. Her eyes were animated with anger. He laughed softly and made a small gesture of defeat. He had conceded the point, and she glanced back at him with an aggrieved look. I wondered how they thought I was taking all this. I tried to imagine my father making that small gesture of defeat, and the image was so unlikely that I was unable to restrain a chuckle. They both looked at me, and I saw in their eyes that they thought I was laughing at their little drama.

'Will you be staying with us long?' Salma asked after the briefest of silences.

I looked towards Bwana Ahmed, hoping he would provide a hint of my prospects. He looked away, glancing towards the kitchen door. 'Why don't we go to the living-room? Ali will bring the coffee in there, when he remembers. Come.'

As he rose from the table he glanced at my hand, caked now with grease and saffron. They had used spoons. A brief look of disgust crossed his face. 'Excuse me,' I said and hurried away to the bathroom to wash. I looked in the mirror and wondered how long I would have to put up with being a guest at Bwana Ahmed bin Khalifa's house and home. They were talking about Ali when I went back.

'He likes you,' Salma said. 'You were in favour, I think ...'

'He's been smoking hashish again,' Bwana Ahmed said impatiently. 'He smokes every evening.'

Ali came in with the coffee. He seemed to be in a hurry, depositing the tray on the table and leaving without a word. Father and daughter exchanged a look, and Bwana Ahmed shook his head. 'He'll go and beat his wife now. When something happens ... your arrival today ... he smokes too much and behaves like a fool. Then he beats his wife, poor woman. That's all they know ... hashish, women and violence. Then they think they can govern the country.'

Salma rose and poured the coffee. 'Black or white?' she asked in English. I must have looked mystified. She smiled, remembering as I did the way I had introduced myself in the morning. 'Do you want milk in your coffee?' she asked.

'No thank you,' I said hesitantly, anxious not to fail another test.

'Try it,' Uncle Ahmed insisted. 'Milk and sugar – it makes coffee taste very nice. Not like that bitter stuff you drink on the coast. Try some ... Give him some, Salma.' She gave me a cup containing a murky, revolting-tasting liquid. I smacked my lips and hummed with pleasure as I sipped

112

it. She smiled while her father raised his eyes to heaven at my ignorance.

She rose to select a book from the shelf behind me, and stood behind my chair, turning the pages slowly. I was thrilled by her intimacy as she casually performed such an ordinary action. She returned to her chair, moved it a little to catch the light and busied herself with her comfort. From where I was sitting the title looked like *Selected Plains*. She spread the book out on her curled-up lap, slotted her fist under her chin and buried herself away.

Bwana Ahmed hissed tunelessly through half-closed lips, looking ahead of him. Then suddenly, like a man inspired, he rose and switched on the radio. He rummaged among a pile of books and brought out a photo album. He gave it to me without a word but with a broad smile. We spent what was left of the evening looking at the photographs. There were no pictures of Salma's mother, and Bwana Ahmed made no references to her.

It was still early when Salma decided she would go to bed. She passed out of the room with a quiet goodnight. I was sorry to see her go. Even sitting quietly in her chair she was a comfort. I found it more difficult to repress the yawns after she had gone. In the end, Bwana Ahmed apologised for keeping me up so late after a long journey and insisted that I go to bed. I left him cradling his photo album, absorbed in the search for his pipe.

I woke up with the sun in my eyes. A window was open and I smelt the moisture in the air. Whichever way I lay, the bed was soft and yielding. The sheets were still a little stiff with newness, and had faint traces of perfume. A muted bird-call drifted through the mesh on the window. The air was filled with the smell of green sap in the growing plants outside. I was reluctant to move, drifting through the memory of the dream I had woken from.

The fine mesh across the window broke the force of the sun, scattering the light around the room, adding to the room's unreality. I turned over and closed my eyes. A car drew near, crunched across the front of the house and raced past. I felt I could lie there for ever, hiding from the business that had brought me to this sanctuary.

I could not imagine myself asking Bwana Ahmed for money. I had seen enough to guess that he would not give me anything. I knew that he held me in some contempt, not so much for something I had done or said, but for what I was there for, for what I was. I did not imagine that my clowning at the table had made any difference one way or another, except perhaps to make him suspicious of me. His anger with Salma's brief interest in what I had said was not because he feared for her virtue, or that he assumed that I had come secretly to court my rich cousin. If he had feared that he would have asked me to leave immediately. I think he wanted to maintain an atmosphere of hostility and rejection, to be hospitable and correct, but to close off the routes that would allow me to ask the favour I had come for. That was why Salma had pretended ignorance of my arrival. I could not believe that it had all been planned, but I could imagine Bwana Ahmed saying to Salma, *He's come here to ask for money. So don't encourage him.* And I could imagine Salma, in her composed and self-confident way, relishing the prospect of gently cutting country boy down to size. Why had he not just said no?

I had thought that if my uncle proved difficult I would have to mention – *though it pains me, ami yangu, to raise the matter at all* – my mother's inheritance. Having seen the man, and had a taste of his smug superiority, I did not think

I could do that now. Perhaps it was because of the inheritance that he had invited me, to see if it was still an issue, to see if I would raise it. I could picture the contempt with which he would dismiss such presumption. The poor relation had not come to ask a favour, after all, but to demand some imagined right of inheritance.

Then I began to think that perhaps I was being unkind to them. What else could he do with my father's letter? Perhaps he thought I would enjoy the holiday. I began to feel guilty for the trouble I was causing them. I was an embarrassment, and all that my clowning had done was to make them pity and despise me. They could have treated me worse. I had no illusions about that. I think I would have gladly left had I known a way of doing so without seeming foolish to my parents.

There was no one in the kitchen when I got there. The room was brightly painted in shades of blue. Cupboards ran along the walls, and an aluminium sink glistened under the window. Two tall fridges stood side by side just inside the back door. I marvelled at the cleanliness and order in everything, and smiled to myself as a picture of the smoke-blackened hole in the backyard of our house presented itself for comparison. It did not surprise me that I had seen no sign of any cockroaches in the house. What would they eat? I could not see any food.

Stoppered glass jars stood on a shelf by the window, reminiscent of the rows of specimen jars on the laboratory benches at school, containing what looked like lumps of corpses pickled in murky brine. I wondered if a search through the cupboards might yield some bread. I found a tin of coffee. I was sitting down at the checked formica table, more shades of blue, waiting for the water to boil, when Ali came in through the back door. He looked coldly

115

at me for a moment, too surprised to have decided on a face. I saw him consider whether to take umbrage at my presence, and then he grinned.

'Some more biriani?' he asked.

He offered me eggs for breakfast. He was wearing ragged bermuda shorts and an aged tennis shirt. The back of his left calf was disfigured by an enormous scar, and I noticed that he avoided putting his whole weight on the left leg. He bustled around me, emptying the pan I had put on the stove and filling up a kettle. He brought out a carton of eggs from the cupboard and asked me if I wanted cow's-eye or scrambled. Cow's-eye, he explained, was a fried egg with the yolk unbroken. It was a rare pleasure to eat eggs and my mouth watered in anticipation.

'They've gone to town,' he said, turning to smile at me. 'They waited ... but you were sleeping. You like sleeping, eh? It's late. Two days a week Miss Salma goes to work and Bwana does not like to be late.'

He smiled again, understanding but not absolving me of blame for having stayed in bed late. 'The journey must've been tiring,' he said. I guessed he must be nearly forty, thin and wasted, but with a reserve that gave him some dignity. I could not imagine him beating his wife. He seemed that morning such a hopeless, defeated man, affecting an interest in a guest he was allowed to dislike. He was frying the eggs with a jaunty air. *There's nothing I like better than to fry up some eggs for a young guest who stays in bed until after eleven o'clock*. He showed me half a face now and then, eagle-eyed at the greasy, sweating pan.

'I've never been to the coast,' he said. 'I've heard a lot ... It's only a day's journey but I can never find the time. Do you want your eggs turned over? I'll bring your breakfast in the dining-room if you want.' He talked in a mixture of

116

English and Kiswahili, the Kiswahili gradually gaining the upper hand.

'I'll eat in here,' I offered. 'If that's all right? Can I have some bread?'

'*Ehe, ehe*,' he said, moving swiftly to turn off the kettle. He poured me a coffee and placed it in front of me. He sliced a whole loaf and put it in front of me before serving me my eggs. 'I've heard a lot of things,' he said, glancing at me from under heavy eyebrows. 'Very interesting.' He said this kindly, reassuringly, moving away towards the sink.

The eggs were delicious. Ali had poured milk in the coffee. I sipped it with resignation. 'I've heard that people on the coast are civilised,' he said, beaming an obsequious smile. I laughed. His face twitched, as if an internal pain had flashed across it.

'People say things like that,' I said, thinking I had wounded him.

'But it's true, no?'

'These eggs are lovely,' I said.

'That's all right,' he said, offhand. 'A friend told me. He said people are very civilised. He said they are never rough or rude.' I wondered if he was playing a game with me. There was so much that was not being said. He must have met people from the coast, must have known that his friend was being too generous. Perhaps he simply meant that the people on the coast were foreigners, and he was performing the kindness of telling me how much better foreignness must be in order to put me at my ease.

'Does your friend come from the coast?' I asked.

'No,' he said, grinning as if he had caught me out in an argument. 'No, no, no. He comes from Tororo, but he was on the coast for many years. He told me there were some rogues' – brushing away a minor blemish – 'but he said the real coast people are different ... kind and civilised.'

'I think your friend was lying,' I said.

A small frown of irritation passed across his brow. I sensed him withdrawing, looking at me again. Then a new look of malice came into his eyes. 'You say he tells lies. He said some bad things.' He hesitated, not with the pained uncertainty that he was trying to suggest he felt, but with caution, testing the ground before approaching his victim. I smiled encouragingly, inviting his malice, eager for the humiliation. He cleared the dirty plates, stoking his grievance. When he turned back to me, his smile had a theatrical anxiety, as if in apology for the hurtful things he was forced to say.

'He said they are clever people. They cheat you all the time but you can't call it thieving.' He smiled again, and I waited. I suppose I knew what he was going to say. 'There are many Arabs there.' He hesitated again, revulsion rising on his face. 'He said men and men have sex. You know, they enter each other through the back, like dogs.'

He was sitting down now, across the table from me. He shook his head slowly, angling his face away from me. 'It's dirty ... like animals!' His brow was furrowed as if he was filled with horror and amazement, but his eyes were bright with pleasure. He looked at me for an explanation. When I gave none, he shook his head, mouth slightly open. 'Men are not like that,' he said. 'What do they do with these men? Do they put them in prison?'

For a terrible moment I wondered if Ali had been instructed to do this. I thought of my father and his shame, and I wished I could leave that house and return to them, and tell them that we deserved no better. The whole world holds us in contempt. Ali went back to the sink to do the washing-up, smiling to himself. I made myself another cup of coffee, without milk this time. 'I hear,' he said, his voice lowered, 'that the white woman does it with her dog. I hear they let them lick their bodies. A friend who worked for a European told me that. Do you think it's true? He said she had marks all over her.'

I shrugged and smiled at him. His huge eyes stared blankly at me. The brief spell of abandonment to malice was now over, shielded behind this blameless neutrality. 'It'll rain today,' he said.

The memory cut through to the bone. *There'll be rain tonight*, she had said, as we sat in the backyard that night making up this fantasy. I went outside into the garden. The hills rolled away in front of me, rising and receding into the far distance. The light was less brazen here than at home, more subdued. I strolled towards the trees, following the chalked lines of the badminton court. Over the back fence were large fields covered with tall, brown grass. In the distance the hills seemed to disappear into a haze, as if they became part of the sky. Near the fence, unconcerned by my presence, were two crown birds. I stopped for a long while, looking at them. In the end their eyes grew suspicious. As their necks moved agitatedly, the light fell off their shiny, grey plumage in sparklets of yellow and green.

I walked back to the trees and stretched out under the shade of a sufi tree. I woke up with a start, surprised that I had fallen asleep yet again. The sky above me had changed. The sun was no longer shining through the trees and the playful, scattered specks of cloud had gone, swallowed up by a huge, dirty mass, threatening in appearance. The air was heavy, like the breath of a hothouse. Like ectoplasm, the clouds were in motion. There was an expectant silence in the air. A sharp scream floated in from the distance. It seemed to be coming from the hills.

I waited for the rain. I felt an overpowering lethargy, defeated. When the rain came, it was sudden and malevolently intense. I let it hit me for a few moments, drinking strength from its power. Then I rose and ran for the house, taking the steps to the terrace in two bounding leaps.

I was in my room when they came back late in the afternoon. I saw Salma walk round the corner of the hedge and down the path to the house. Her hair was out of its tight knot, and was combed back. It made her face look leaner, harder. I think she glanced at my window out of the corner of her eye, and perhaps she saw me there. Bwana Ahmed drove up a little later. I went out to the living-room so they should not think me solitary and rude. Bwana Ahmed was in a bad temper. I heard his voice coming from the kitchen. Salma was on the terrace, sipping a soft drink and looking out across the rain-sodden fields.

'Had a good rest?' she asked. She looked tired and miserable.

'Excellent,' I said, sitting on the terrace wall beside her. 'I went out there this morning and I fell asleep under that sufi tree. Look, you can still see my coffee cup out there.'

She shook her head at me and smiled. 'You must have a disease or something,' she said.

'It's the air up here.'

'I must go and have a wash,' she said. She put her glass down on the terrace wall and walked away. Bwana Ahmed walked past, calling out a greeting. 'Hassan, you're awake at last.'

'I'm on holiday, aren't I?' I called back.

Bwana Ahmed said he would have only a light supper, and Ali had to go back to the kitchen and rethink the meal. It was quite early when he called us to the table, daylight still filtering in through the dining-room window.

'Where is he? He rushes us in here and then keeps us waiting. That man's an idiot. Ali!' Bwana Ahmed leant back in his chair, waiting for Ali to answer his call.

Salma rested her face on her hand, her elbow on the table. The light from the window threw the faint down on her upper lip into relief. I sensed that Bwana Ahmed's eyes had come to rest on me.

'The rain seems to have stopped,' I said to her.

She nodded but did not say anything. Bwana Ahmed's fingers were drumming furiously on the table. He clucked angrily, on the verge of rising. I glanced at Salma. She was sitting up, poised to move. At a second, explosive *cluck*, she stood up and hurried round the table. Ali strolled in through the door, carrying a tureen pressed to his chest.

'What have you been doing?' demanded the angry Master. He glanced at his watch and looked round the table for sympathy. We sat silently while Ali measured out the soup and placed a bowl in front of each of us. I feared to swallow in the silence, taking tiny sips of the soup and keeping firm control of the movements of my Adam's apple. Bwana Ahmed left as soon as he had taken his last spoonful of soup, mumbling a perfunctory *Excuse me*.

Salma sighed. 'I don't think it's been a good day.'

'How was your day? I hear you've been to work.' I looked at her as I spoke, and I saw the muscles round her mouth relax a little. She still looked miserable. 'What kind of work do you do?'

'I just work part time in a bookshop,' she said, tucking her hands under the table. 'I wanted a year off before I started at the University. Daddy thinks I'm stupid, but I didn't want to just go on from school to university ... like going through a machine. I wanted to do something different.'

121

'Like working in a bookshop.'

'Yes, I know. It's very tame, isn't it? If I was a man I would have found myself a job on an upland farm, or signed up as a sailor,' she said, smiling.

'How about a big-game hunter?' I suggested.

'Very funny,' she said. 'You don't know how hard it was to persuade Daddy to let me work at all. He said people would talk. In the end he got me the job at the bookshop, just to keep me quiet. It's not ... very adventurous, but it's better than nothing. Anyway, I wonder what else Ali has got for us to eat?'

'Not another biriani, I hope.'

She made a face when I said that. I realised that I had spoken the words as a kind of apology, and the face was a way of dismissing the subject as of no importance.

'Will you be going to Nairobi University next year?'

She nodded.

'I met somebody who's a student here,' I said. 'We came together on the train.'

'He must be a postgraduate,' she said after a moment of thought. 'The students went on holiday last week.'

I was getting a new angle on Moses Mwinyi. He would not have neglected to tell me if he was a postgraduate student. I was looking forward even more to meeting him again.

'Did you finish school this year?' she asked me.

'Yes,' I said. 'The same time as you.'

'Were your results all right?'

I explained that the results had not been released by the government. Once I started I found myself unable to stop. She listened to me without saying a word. She smiled when I insisted that I was sure that I had done very well, but it did not seem like mockery. Ali interrupted us with a dish of water-beans and a plateful of parathas. He made a comical face at Salma and she grinned, no longer tense, and shook her head to stop him from saying anything about Bwana Ahmed.

'So things have become very difficult now?' she asked after he had gone.

'Yes,' I said, unwilling to enter the conversation.

'Discrimination?' she asked. The word sounded innocent, spoken by somebody who had not yet experienced its full squalor. I sensed some scepticism in her tone, some reluctance to credit the response that she expected me to make.

'Something like that,' I said.

'Like what?' she asked, frowning.

'Like ... yes. There is discrimination. People are victimised because they don't have a black skin. It's revenge. They are paying back what they owe. People are afraid. Harsh things happen. Cruel things are done. I think it hurts everybody in the end. I think it's bad for everybody. We all end up being a little less human.'

I felt her resistance. I returned to the parathas and beans. We were silent for a while, then she began to talk about the war in Nigeria. *Such a stable country ... what's Africa coming to ... we'll end up like Latin America.* Bwana Ahmed coughed in the living-room. Salma stopped instantly, surprised as I was that he had been sitting in there all the time. She mouthed: *We'd better go in.*

'I think I'll go for a walk,' I said after we had finished eating.

Bwana Ahmed looked up from his sheaf of papers as I walked through, but he said nothing. I hesitated, wanting to stop and explain. I felt that they wanted me out of the way, that there were things they needed to say to each other.

It was damp outside. I walked in the deep darkness, astonished by the noise of the night. I had grown up in a

123

town, alleyways to the left and right, where crickets and cicadas skulked in corners of rooms and cheeped tentatively. In rural Nairobi they were in full song, scratching the night air with abandon. I walked for a long time, lit part of the way by the yard lights of the great houses I passed. It was the dogs that turned me back, a pack of scavengers which stopped its work and regarded me with more than passing interest. When I got back I found that the terrace door had been left unlocked. Neither Salma nor her father were about, but there was a tension in the air, a disturbance, and I guessed that they had fought in my absence. I hoped it had been about me.

I heard a woman scream and I went out to the kitchen to see what was going on. I assumed that Ali was exercising his manhood. I stood in the dark, looking out of the glass door, wondering if I would be able to distinguish the shape and power of Ali's fist as it landed on his wife's face.

In bed I could only think of Salma. Whatever was to happen to me in years to come, I knew that I would never forget her. I lay in bed and wondered what it must feel like to be wanted by a girl like her. I imagined her turning to me in the morning and asking me to run off to the Ruwenzori with her ... even to the Bahr el Ghazal ... or all the way to Alexandria. I wanted to ask her about her mother, and the silence about her.

I had intended to be up early, to show willing, but I found that Bwana Ahmed had already left. I had thought to ask him for a lift to town and for directions to the University. Talking of Moses with Salma had reminded me how much I had enjoyed him, how he had seemed alive and uncomplicated. I wanted to see if he had really lied to me about being a student. It did not matter very much about the lie, even seemed in character. It would have tripped from his tongue with the facility of practice, fulfilling the needs of the moment. Going to see him was also going to be a way of declaring my independence, to show that I had my own complicated life outside the begging-mission that I was on.

I found Ali sitting at the kitchen table, fast asleep. I tried to tiptoe out again, but he stirred and sucked back the long thread of saliva that was dangling out of his mouth. Without needing the time to shake the sleep out of his head, rub his eyes with balled fists or lazily scratch his belly, he grinned. He got up without a word, grinning, and started to fry me an egg.

'I hear there are a lot of big shops on the coast,' he said, stifling a yawn.

I ran away to the living-room. I heard Ali behind me hiss with surprise. It was raining again, and I stood by the open glass doors, watching the fine, slanting strokes line the air, feeling as if I was in prison.

'Isn't it beautiful?' asked Salma. She was wearing a scarf round her neck, of a yellow, brown and red stripe design, knotted to one side with the two ends hanging down like floppy ears on either side of her shoulder. Her hair was pulled off her face as it had been the first time I had seen her. She stood beside me at the open door, leaning against the door frame like the bad girl in an old movie. 'Look at the fields. Aren't they beautiful? Don't they look romantic?' She glanced over her shoulder at Genghis Khan, who was standing in the archway looking wounded. 'Ali, are there people on the hills? Are there people living on the hills? You don't know? Daddy says nobody lives there, but I'm sure he's wrong.'

'I don't know, Miss,' he grumbled, determined to show his hurt. 'Your breakfast is ready, Mr Hassan.'

Salma glanced at me for a second, trying to catch the note of grievance in Ali's voice. It was that look that confirmed that the bright thing was acting out a game whose purpose I did not yet understand.

'Have you ever been there, Ali?' she asked in her new breathless voice. She seemed to be in the grip of a wonderful discovery, and paused to catch her breath, taking in a deep draught of the hill air. Ali glanced at me, was inclined to smile but resisted the temptation. He lowered his eyes without making an answer. 'Perhaps we could go there while you're here,' she said, whipping round to me. 'Would you like to? We could take a picnic.'

To the ends of the earth! To rumble storms in their coming … all the way to Alexandria! No fire nor desert shall stand in our path … anywhere, except on muddy tracks to see little homesteads of suspicious farmers scratching a living out of barren hillsides. The rain, lashing across the empty fields and sky, looked beautiful enough from where I was.

'No, I don't think I'd like to go,' I said.

She laughed. 'No, nor would I. We'll only find that people do live there,' she said, walking ahead of me to the dining-room. 'They'll stare at us and answer our questions with angry grumbles, and try to sell us something we don't want. Anyway, I wasn't serious. Listen, I'll be going to town later, to see a friend at the University, and I thought you might want to come, to look up your friend.' She smiled as she said this, but I sensed the apprehension, as if she was afraid I would turn down her invitation or perhaps misunderstand it. I was grateful that she was trying to be so bright and cheerful, trying to make me feel welcome.

'I'd love to go,' I said. 'That's exactly what I was thinking of doing … '

We sat at the table, and Ali gently, but with an averted face, slid an egg on a plate towards me. He brought her a grapefruit, sliced in half and cut away from the pith.

'I don't want to look fat by the time I'm thirty,' she said, catching my surprised glance at the despised fruit. 'It's in the family. Look at Daddy. We're all like that.' She smiled distantly, as if something entirely different was going through her head.

'Your aunt … my mother, she's not fat,' I said.

She shook her head and then looked away, discouraging me from asking the obvious question about her mother. 'We'll have to wait until the rain stops before we can go,' she said.

In the end we left while it was still raining. She saw the bus pull up at the stop near the house, and she ran out, waving and shouting for me to hurry. I think she was anxious to leave before Bwana Ahmed came home for lunch.

'We don't have much time,' she said when we were on the bus. 'I just want to buy a couple of things … a present for my friend Mariam … and you need a new pair of shoes, I think. Then we'll go to Mariam's.'

'Won't Mariam like my shoes?' I asked.

'Mariam will love them. She's a romantic like that, very impractical. She doesn't like anything that's usual, or normal. Her family live in Nairobi, but she insisted on taking a room at the University. You'll see, she thinks she's a great rebel … and always wants to do what everybody else doesn't want. She drives everybody mad.'

'She sounds nice,' I said.

We went to Kenyatta Avenue, barging through the crowds and arguing with the pavement-sellers. The pavements were slushy with mud, and crowded with people tripping and kicking each other. An insistent street-seller took a shine to me, and persistently tried to unload a gold-plated Seiko wrist-watch on me. Salma encouraged him, telling him that I was the son of one of the richest men in Lamu. In the end we escaped into River Road, and went into every haberdasher's shop down that street. I was conscious most of all of being with her, brushing against her now and then, relishing the appeals she made for my opinion. I enjoyed being authoritative about the texture of a piece of material or the vulgarity of its design. She egged me on, discomfiting the traders and forcing them to drop the price, only to appeal for their sympathy in the end when I still refused to be convinced. Now and then I caught the tail-end of a lingering look, and I wondered if I was over-playing my role. She insisted I try on several pairs of shoes that I knew were beyond my means. I bought a pair of plimsolls: made in Hong Kong.

We went into a boutique – coloured lights and tinsel hanging off the ceiling – where all the clothes had a foreign label and the prices were laughably unreal. Salma bought a scarf for Mariam. *At least you know it's quality*, she said, showing me the Marks & Spencer label. There was a café in the shop and we stopped to have an ice-cream. The ice-cream came in large, canoe-shaped dishes and was smeared and sprinkled with fruit sauces and nuts. In the middle of the concoction stood a bar of Flake, looking in that context like a hardened lump of faeces. I tried not to laugh, for Salma seemed to be eyeing her colourful barge with serious interest. My steely resolve collapsed as I conveyed the first spoonful towards my mouth, and I shot ice-cream and nuts all over the table as I succumbed to a fit of hysterics.

I tried everything. I shut my eyes, I asked for a straw ... I watched Salma eating hers with relish but I could not eat that ice-cream. We left the shop with Salma's reproaches ringing in my ears. *That's the most expensive ice-cream in all Nairobi. Didn't you see all those white people eating in there? And you spit it all over the table.* The ice-cream was called Hawaiian Suntan, and whenever I got myself under control, Salma would say the name and start me off again.

'It's too late to go to Mariam's now,' she said as we walked back to Kenyatta Avenue. 'If you hadn't taken so long over your Hawaiian Suntan ... '

Bwana Ahmed was already home when we got in, late in the afternoon. It was clear he disapproved, although he smiled and asked us about our trip. There was an edge to his smile and an undertone of mockery in his questions. Later in the evening, led on by encouraging nods and smiles from Salma, I talked about home, about the coast, about my parents. He said very little, but he sneered openly and sometimes glanced angrily at Salma. I don't think he realised how completely his face revealed his feelings. I was sure that the argument had been about me the previous evening, with Salma coming to my defence. I could not understand what Bwana Ahmed could have taken exception to. He had invited me and I had come. What was the fuss about? I was determined now that I was not going to be chased away by his rudeness. He might not give me any money, but I would get my holiday.

Even as I thought that at the time, I suspected that I was missing the point, that I was only incidentally the cause of the tension and that there were other things going on that I did not yet understand. In the end Bwana Ahmed sighed and dropped his eyes. Salma glanced at him, and it was impossible to miss the flash of anxiety in her eyes. I wrapped up my account as speedily as I could and fled.

I found Salma in the kitchen the next morning, talking to Ali. He was pounding and kneading dough with the inattention of long practice, leaning a little towards her as she spoke.

'I'll bring your breakfast,' he said abruptly, as soon as he saw me, inviting me out of the kitchen.

Salma laughed, encouraging the stupid fart in his childish sulks, I thought. How could she laugh at a man who could fry an egg in his sleep and nightly beat the shit out of his wife? I went back to the living-room to ponder this betrayal. He rushed me through breakfast, explaining to Salma that he was very busy.

'He's baking,' she explained.

'What?'

'Bread, just ordinary bread,' she said.

'*Boflo*, we call it on the coast.'

Boflo. The word suddenly brought back a memory of home. The fishermen cleaning their dug-outs and watering their nets, punching holes in the water which flashed up like fragments of light. Wave-crests rearing out of the green sea. Weeds washed up on the beach like sunburnt dreams, washed and left, sinking into the wet, porous sand. In the distance a tiny boat bobs and bucks on the surface, frantic and purposeless. A log of sea-salted wood lies rotting, disembowelled, on the beach, laid open like the belly of a dolphin.

I thought of the first time I had seen her, the blouse tight across her chest, her shoulder-blades rising against her tautened skin, frightening me with her unrelenting self-control. Now she sat back in her chair with a heavy sigh. She looked up and waited a moment as if gathering resolve. 'Were you angry with us last night?' she asked.

'Was he angry because of me?' I enquired.

'No, not really,' she said, looking pained. 'It's difficult to explain … but … sometimes he makes things look worse than they really are.'

130

'Is it because I'm here?'

'No, I don't think so,' she said after a long time.

She wanted me to know that she was lying. She was trying to tell me that I had failed. I was not even saddened by it. I was more saddened by the thought of losing her friendship, her companionship, even though I understood that her attention arose out of his treatment of me.

'Why did he ask me to come?' I asked.

She looked away, and I thought then that it was wrong of me to test her loyalties in that way. I did not take the question back, and we sat in silence while it dissipated itself. A bee flew into the room, and she stood up, watching it. It flung itself against the radio then fell to the floor, its wings buzzing with distress. She ran to the kitchen and returned with a broom, shoving it towards me with a smile. I took the broom and smashed it against the bee. Its belly broken, oozing white pus, it slowly stretched itself in relief. Its sting moved in and out of its socket like an animal aroused. Its eyes stared mildly out of its unbending body.

'I just wanted you to sweep it out,' she said.

She walked across to the radio and turned it on. An English voice was speaking of the early Christian missions in Uganda: *Colonial administrators manipulated local, regional and ethnic differences* ... She switched the radio off.

'Let's go,' she said. 'Let's see if we can catch Mariam today.'

I was surprised by the emptiness of the place. She had told me that the students were on holiday, but I had not expected the tomb-like silence of the buildings or the dreariness of the deserted grounds. Mariam was a graduate assistant at the University, staying on during the holidays to complete her dissertation. Salma told me it was something to do with the history of art.

We walked up grubby stairs and down a long corridor of closed doors, all painted green. There was a smell of dust and damp, mingled with old sweat. We found Mariam in her room. She was a short, plump girl who talked very quickly and was quick to smile. She was obviously delighted to see Salma, holding on to her hand as they greeted each other and exchanged news. Her room was scattered with canvases and sketches, some hanging on the walls, others pinned to the bookshelf, some thrown carelessly on the floor. It looked as I had imagined a student's room would, and I was filled with a familiar envy.

When Salma introduced us, she looked me up and down then nodded her approval. We grinned at each other as we shook hands.

'So you're the relative from the coast, with plenty of brains but no money,' she said, glancing at Salma. 'I've heard about you. I hope she's been showing you the sights.'

I told her about the Hawaiian Suntan and she looked disapproving and cross. *You're such a philistine, Salma.* She offered, eyebrows raised archly, to show me the sights. I asked her about the paintings, enquiring if she had done them all. She wound herself up and talked enthusiastically about what she was trying to do as she took me round her small gallery. She talked about lines and despair and loneliness, and I tried to act the way I imagined a sophisticated, cultured character in a novel might. I asked questions about influences and the function of art. She talked at such speed that at times she ran short of breath. I did not understand everything she said, but it sounded very good and I nodded as if I shared her views. She drew me to a large painting to illustrate what she was saying. It consisted of a broken chair, lying abandoned on its side. Beside it lay a hat and a leaking fountain-pen. In the background were weirdly elongated figures, slithering through misty shadows. It was called *Betrayal*.

'Is this modern art?' I asked.

'I'm not sure that it's art at all,' she said. 'It's only what I do. It's up to whoever looks at it to decide whether it is art or not.'

'Of course it's art,' said Salma, giving me a sharp look of rebuke. 'Somebody offered how much for it, Mariam?'

'It doesn't matter,' said Mariam, laughing. 'You really are a philistine, Salma. *How much* would not make it art.'

'What would, then?' asked Salma.

Mariam hissed with exaggerated surprise. She glanced at me for sympathy and then shrugged. She took me to another work, which she told me was derived from a famous painting by Picasso, whom she counted the supreme master. Did I not agree? Although for ideas she found the works of Tolkien truly inspiring ... I confessed that I had heard of neither. They were astonished, exclaiming that they would not have thought it possible. I saw the scales falling off Mariam's eyes, and I saw her looking at me again, as if she was seeing me for the first time.

They relieved me of my ignorance over lunch at a nearby Indian café. I resisted, making difficulties, refusing to be impressed. In the end, Salma was so provoked that she slapped me on the thigh. 'What do you people on the coast know? You're just sailors and fishermen,' she said. I treasured that slap while the two of them ranted on about my ignorance.

They came with me to the administration offices to ask about Moses, but no one there knew the name.

Bwana Ahmed took my side when Salma gleefully retold the story of my ignorance. 'Why should he know about those crazy people? What have they done that's so important?' Salma put up a vigorous defence but Bwana Ahmed insistently repeated his last question. *What have they done that's so important? Tell me that. You can't, can you? What have they done that's so important?* She gave up in the end, raising her eyes to heaven and praying for patience.

'Don't let them make you feel ignorant,' he said, turning to me. 'It's all fashion to them. Picasso! Who's Picasso? You have a good time and don't let them worry you. Tomorrow they'll say somebody else is a genius.'

'Daddy, you're making yourself sound ignorant,' she said with a pitying look. He made a face, dismissing her criticism, and then flashed a grin of complicity at me.

'I waited for you today,' he said, sounding wounded but looking pleased with himself. 'I thought you might want to go to the Juma'a mosque for Friday prayers.' He took me out that evening. He told me this was his regular Friday outing.

'I've been going there for years,' he said as we drove to town. 'We gather at Thabit Adnan's house and just greet each other and talk. Thabit comes from the coast. I don't know if you know his family. He's very rich now, most of it from smuggling and foreign exchange deals. But he's a good man, a very gentle man.'

It was a splendid town-house, looming all of a sudden out of a narrow road and surrounded by smaller houses that nestled contentedly around it. The gathering was all male, and was dominated by conversation about money and politics. Thabit Adnan fed us like kings, and stoked the fires of contention whenever the conversation became too tame. Bwana Ahmed told him about me.

'A compatriot of yours ... he's visiting us from the coast.'

'You're welcome,' said the gracious man. 'Is your family well? Your father and your mother? Everybody at home? *Alhamdulillah*! There's nothing there now. You should get your uncle to give you a job here in Nairobi. There are still opportunities here.'

I glanced at Bwana Ahmed to see how he was taking this suggestion. He shrugged. 'There's a job if he wants one. But these young people don't want to do dirty work. They don't even want to do office work. They all want to be professors and geniuses and doctors. Today my daughter tells me that Picasso is a genius. Who's Picasso? I asked her. What has he done?'

Bwana Ahmed was very cheerful in the car as we drove back later that evening. I began to sense that he was becoming interested in the idea of offering me a job. He did not say anything more but I felt sure he was thinking about it. It was the way he avoided the subject that made me certain. He would have been embarrassed otherwise, but he was acting like somebody with a cheerful secret to divulge, over which he was taking his time.

When we got back to the house we found a little boy standing in the shadows of the drive. Bwana Ahmed got out of the car and went over to speak to him. 'Ali's hurt himself,' he said when he came back. Salma came out of the house, and the two of them exchanged whispered words. They slid into the shadows round the corner of the thorny hedge, and after a moment I heard voices. Salma came back very quickly. 'Help us,' she said.

Ali was lying propped up against the veranda wall of the two-roomed shack that was his house. In the feeble light, I saw a short, round-faced woman standing a few feet from him, watching his abandoned body with indifference. The little boy had gone to stand beside the woman. We dragged

Ali into the light while the woman watched us. He had cut himself down the arm, and the gash revealed the whiteness of bone near the elbow. He seemed to be unconscious.

'Who did this?' I asked, my stomach turning at the sight of so much blood.

'He did,' said Bwana Ahmed, his voice unusually low and pained.

'To himself! I've never seen so much blood.'

'He smokes too much,' Salma said, glancing quickly at the woman. 'Then he does this. We must hurry, Daddy. Look at Mali,' she glanced again at the woman. 'She goes into a daze like this when he hurts himself. Mali, that's his wife.'

I helped them put Ali in the car. The woman followed us at a respectful distance. Salma sat with him in the back while Mali stood on the road and watched them drive away. I became aware that I was alone with her. I felt that I should say something comforting, but I was so astonished by the squalor of her existence that I could only hurry back inside, filled with shame and fear. She made me think of my mother and Zakiya.

I waited up for a while, but I could not stay awake. They found me asleep in the chair when they came back. I woke up to find Bwana Ahmed leaning over me, shaking me gently. 'It's three o'clock,' he said. 'Go to bed.' Salma was smiling, her arms folded across her chest.

'I fell asleep,' I said. Bwana Ahmed helped me up, laughing at me. 'How was he?' I asked.

'It's bad round the elbow,' Salma said. 'But otherwise he's not too bad.'

'He'll survive, the bloody idiot,' said Bwana Ahmed.

'They'll let him out tomorrow,' said Salma. 'Then Mali will look after him. She always does that, goes into a daze.

He's terrible … the things he does. He beats her then does this … mutilates himself.'

'He'll kill himself, or her, one of these days,' Bwana Ahmed said bitterly. 'Come on, bed. Everybody bed. I'll go and tell Mali.'

We played badminton the next day. Bwana Ahmed was the best of us, and the least restrained in his enjoyment. When he came out to suggest the game he was already changed into sports shorts and T-shirt. He raced round the grass court chasing everything with a podgy dignity, never seeming to strain. He taunted us with our poor shots, until in the end Salma rushed round to his side of the court and smacked him with a racket. Left alone with me, Bwana Ahmed lost his appetite for slaughter. We sat on the terrace and sipped cold drinks, turning in our silences to all the things we had not been talking about.

'You're going to work on Monday, Salma?' he asked after a desperate silence. She nodded. 'I thought Hassan could come with me on Monday … to the showroom. Come and see what we do here. In case he wants to stay and take the job I've offered him.'

'What job?' she asked.

He explained and she smiled encouragement. I could see that they were pleased with each other. Honour was saved. I was not to be sent away empty-handed. They expected me to say no, I was sure of that. It felt dishonourable to accept, as if it would be taking advantage of their kind gesture.

Salma spent the afternoon in the kitchen, preparing the dinner. Bwana Ahmed went to take a nap. I sat in the living-room looking through the pile of books. Sometimes Salma came from the kitchen and sat with me for a while. She offered to get her record-player and records, and told me she loved dancing.

137

'What dances can you do?' she asked.

I told her that I had never danced in my life. She did not believe me at first, and then promised to teach me. She looked wisely at me, and thought of saying something but then changed her mind. I knew she wanted me to say something about being offered the job, to admit that it had absolved them their first insensitivity in inviting me here.

'Why is your mother never mentioned?' I asked her when she came again from the kitchen. She glanced down the corridor and shook her head. She did not come in again after that.

On Sunday we went for a drive in the country. They took me to Nairobi Game Park, and Bwana Ahmed pointed out the animals to me as if he owned them. We found Ali at home when we got back, discharged from hospital that afternoon. He was full of smiles and apologies. Bwana Ahmed spent an hour with him in the kitchen before we went out. We had been invited to dinner by one of his friends. It turned out to be an Ethiopian business man and his family. Bwana Ahmed introduced me as a nephew who had come to work for him.

The mother supervised the servants as they laid the food out on the large, shiny table. She did so without saying a word to them but by hovering a few feet from them, her arms folded across her chest. She was silent all the time we were there, and the father egged his two sons and one daughter on, encouraging them to show their paces. The elder brother paid much attention to Salma, promising to visit her at the bookshop the next day. As we were leaving, the mother brought a small packet containing sandalwood and gave it to Salma.

Bwana Ahmed was very pleased with the evening and teased Salma about expecting a proposal from the elder brother. 'They're a very rich family. They have all kinds of businesses. And the young man seemed very nice. I'll get a big dowry out of them. What do you think, Hassan? What shall I tell them when they come to ask for her?'

'Tell them to ask her,' I said, hearing myself speak after hours of silence. Salma applauded me sarcastically.

Bwana Ahmed owned not only a used-car business, but also a fridge and freezer store, and a butcher's shop. We spent the day driving from one to the other for no clearly discernible purpose. He had managers running all three businesses, but he treated them as if they would be lost without his abrupt and barely polite questioning. In between journeys, he made many phone calls cancelling orders, chivvying suppliers and counting huge piles of banknotes.

'I can't trust any of those managers,' he told me, as we raced off with the money to catch the banks before they shut. 'They cheat me all the time. That's why I would like you to come and work here. You could keep an eye on things for me, and then when you've got enough experience, I'll make you one of my managers. You can't trust these Africans. They either steal from you or they let the business go to hell. You go near any of these big shot Africans first thing in the morning you can smell booze on their breath. You can't trust them.'

When we got to the bank he disappeared into an inner office for an hour or so. I waited in the car, watching the traffic of cars and bicycles rush noisily past.

'They won't give me enough foreign,' he said when he came back. 'Let's get a Coke and then we'll have to go and buy some dollars.'

We tried several places. At all of them Bwana Ahmed was treated with great respect and taken to inner rooms while I waited outside. In the end he said we would have to go to the tourist traps, the big hotels. He had got most of the money changed, but he was still a few hundred short. I asked him what he needed the foreign exchange for.

'Where do you think those cars come from? Do you think my suppliers will accept this Monopoly money we use here?'

We drove into a palm-fringed car-park of a large tourist hotel. Sitting on a bench under one of the palm trees was Moses Mwinyi. My uncle walked directly towards him and I followed. Moses recognised me at once and rose to greet me as if we were long-lost friends.

'How are you, my buddy? What do you think of the great city? Is this your father?' He took my hand and held on to it, talking and grinning, while Bwana Ahmed waited. When his joy at seeing me had subsided, he turned to Bwana Ahmed with a more serious, business-like manner. They talked prices and amounts, abused each other with an intense persistence and agreed details of collection and delivery.

'You must come round another day, bro,' Moses said as we were leaving. 'I will buy you some chicken this time. And I can take you on that tour I promised. I'm always here, just ask for Moses Mwinyi.'

From the car I saw Moses being joined by some of the other money-changers who had been watching our transaction from a distance. They slapped hands and laughed as they congratulated Moses.

'How do you know that jackal?' Bwana Ahmed asked as we drove away. He was greatly amused when I told him. 'He's a flunkey, a nobody. He gets a few shillings for taking the risk with somebody else's money. He probably works for some ambassador or something. He's a pimp, he gets women for these tourists. I know him.'

We went back the next day to collect the dollars. Moses chatted happily as we followed him to the hotel curio shop. It was there that the money changed hands. There were no furtive looks around, no bundles of money wrapped in brown paper. The notes changed hands openly, within sight of the hotel reception desk and the two armed policemen lounging near the hotel entrance.

'Don't forget,' Moses insisted as he saw us to the car. 'Any time ... I'm here. Come round for that tour. You promise me now, my bro. Goodbye, Daddy, don't forget me in your will.'

'Somebody should fuck that man's mouth. Do you know what he means by that tour? Do you understand ... '

'Wait a minute,' I said, jumping out of the car and hurrying after Moses. He stopped when he heard me approach and turned to wait for me. His face wore the empty grin of the pitiless hustler.

'I looked for you at the University,' I said.

His grin broadened, but his eyes hardened with suspicion. I wondered if I had done the wrong thing, if he would now mock me for my innocence. Or he might think that I was mocking and chastising him for his lies.

'I go there sometimes,' he said and laughed with the ugly cynicism of the big-city pimp.

'What about killing the tribals? Is this where you are going to do it from?' I laughed too, to make him understand that I was not just being righteous, that I wanted to know.

'Listen,' he said as the grin disappeared from his face. 'This is what I do, and people like you are my customers. I say what I like, and you believe what you like. I don't know what you think ... You want to come and meet me, you'll find me here. This is where I do business.'

141

'Sorry,' I said. 'I just couldn't believe it was the same person I'd met.'

'Fuck off!' he said. 'You don't know anything ... Go back to big daddy. He's waiting for you.'

He called out as I was walking back. He called me a blood-sucker, and I understood what he meant. He meant that I was making him guilty for doing what people like us wanted him to do. That is what he meant by describing me as his customer. As I reached the car I wished I had not just left, but had told him I understood what he meant but that he was wrong to think that. He shouted something else, but I did not hear it. When I turned to look as the car drove away, I saw him standing with his hands on his hips, head thrown back, laughing. I knew the hollowness of that laughter even though I could not hear it.

'What made you go back?' Bwana Ahmed asked. I could tell that he was not angry. His voice was even sympathetic, careful not to cause offence.

'I couldn't believe that that was the same man I had met. I didn't want just to go away ... '

'You liked him,' he said after a long silence. 'It happens sometimes, and then afterwards you can't understand how you could have been so foolish.' He glanced at me and smiled. 'It happens to all of us. Don't worry about him. Let's go and finish this business. I want to put the order in today.'

I spent the rest of the week chasing around Nairobi with Bwana Ahmed. Everywhere he went, he argued with people, and swore as we departed that he would never take his business there again. He spoke of me as his nephew who had come to work for him. I began to feel as if I was something of his, something he owned. The managers of his three businesses treated me with an obsequiousness

I found hard to understand. I had heard Bwana Ahmed say to them in my hearing that I was to take over their jobs. He encouraged a habit of dependence, and persuaded the people who worked for him to be grateful for the patronage he granted them by giving them work. I knew that I would not stay to work for him, but he tempted me with unexpected kindnesses that came in moods and spasms, and spoke of the beginnings of a warmth towards me.

There was also Salma. I saw the pleasure she took in the account her father gave of our day, and the easy manner with which she admitted me into a kind of family intimacy. It was not the kind of intimacy I wanted, and I found myself resisting being cast as a member of the family. I was hardly ever alone with her, but I still found myself playing the hazardous and complicated game of making sure she understood that I was attracted to her. I wonder now where I found the nerve for such boldness.

Bwana Ahmed went out on Saturday afternoon to visit a friend in hospital. I felt a tension as soon as Salma and I were alone. She talked freely, it seemed, but our eyes seemed to meet more often than usual. I found myself getting hot at the reassurance that her manner offered me. I felt myself leaning back with some relief, thinking that I could let things take their course more gently. She went to her room and brought out her record-player. We spent the afternoon listening to old records while Salma told me of times and events connected with them. She taught me how to do the waltz. At least, she held me while I tried to remember where to put my feet. We were careful that our bodies should not touch, but I thrilled at the warmth of an angled arm resting on mine, and the gentle pressure of her hand as it shifted on my shoulder and accidentally brushed the nape of my neck. At the end of the dancing lessons, we shared little smiles of complicity, which Salma accompanied with merciless ana-lyses of my dancing potential.

It was Ali who came in and put an end to our little game. His arm was in a cast, and his wife came to help him in the kitchen, but he still insisted on doing the chores in the house himself. He had come in to draw the curtains. When I noticed him, he was standing in the archway watching us. He smiled and shook his head at our silliness, but I saw a hard, suspicious look in his eyes.

'Is there a party?' he asked, doing some quick and surpris-ingly elegant dance-steps. 'Bwana will be home very soon.'

He walked to the windows to draw the curtains and glanced over his shoulder at Salma, his face turned away from me. She looked a little guilty, and I could guess what his look said to her. I knew I had not vanquished him, that even in my new acceptance in the household he still treated me with ill-concealed dislike. To him I was still the unwel-come guest, and my dancing with Salma was overweening presumption.

I thought about her all the time, and wove detailed fan-tasies about our coming together. I feared she would have been recalled to her senses by Ali's look, so every time she looked at me and spoke without embarrassment, I took new heart. There were times when it all seemed foolish and dangerous, but there seemed no way of stopping what had been started. I tried to think of myself as the conquering hero, who would ravish the daughter of the proud lord and make her love me, and then abandon her. It was a safer fan-tasy than the others I entertained, but the least truthful. If I made love to her, I would be wrong by any understanding of how a guest should act. If I left her too soon, I was afraid I would lose her for ever, and I would never know what it would have been like to know her. Make love to her! I would not even have known where to start. I don't think that my desire for her was as concentrated and hard as that. I wanted her to be with me, smiling in my face, leaning her warmth against my body. I wanted to please her with my cleverness, and have her reward me with her affection.

In the twilight, we would sit in the garden. The slanting sun would set her hair on fire and burnish her skin with red. Every day things became more difficult, and I dreaded the passing of each day. I told myself that it was foolish, cowardly, to deny the fulfilment of what I felt, that I should not resist but lunge joyously into the flood and live the consequences as I could.

Ali watched us now. Sometimes I glanced up to find Bwana Ahmed looking at me, with a thoughtful and worried stare. At those times I felt like leaving, to escape the suspicion and return later under different terms. I did not trust enough in luck to risk that, and I could not leave while so much was still unspoken. As the days passed, this stew of excitement and guilt grew thicker and more enervating. Bwana Ahmed was beginning to find it difficult to talk to me again. It made it worse that I felt I could sympathise with him.

On a Wednesday, during the third week of my stay with them, she asked me to go to town with her. She had arranged to meet Mariam again, and Mariam had asked that I should come too. Bwana Ahmed excused me from accompanying him as usual with a casual wave of the hand. He would have loved to forbid it, but I understood enough now to know that that was not how they lived. I wanted to tell him that I would not be staying, because I thought that he regretted that offer too. I had not found the opportunity yet, and did not want to be rushed away from Nairobi before I was ready. He still talked as if I would stay, but with less satisfaction at his own generosity.

She took me to the bookshop where she worked two days a week. It was a tiny shop in the shadow of a church, crammed with translations of religious works and school textbooks. The manager was young, and very busy, but he still found time to be welcoming and friendly. After that we wandered the streets, looking into shops and stores.

'I don't understand why we're going into these shops,' I complained. 'You don't buy anything. We go in and look at things, and then you argue with the shopkeeper and then we leave. What's the point of it?'

'The point is I enjoy it,' she said, not in the least cast down. 'I like to see what there is.'

I had an unhappy collision with a fruit-seller and his barrow. The man abused me with fierce relish and venom. He gave a historical account of my lineage that left me trembling with real rage and shame. I insisted that we went to Mariam's after that. We found her in her room at the University. She looked tired and unhappy, and explained that the work was not going well. 'However radically I think things out, as soon as I sit down to write, all that comes out is the same competent, safe crap. I want to argue the link between art in Africa and the social reality of its context. And all that comes out is the same pseudo-religious bullshit. I'm just not good enough to do it.'

We made encouraging noises. I wished I could understand the difficulties, that they were my difficulties, that I too could be made unhappy by such failures. I think things became very clear to her very quickly, and the arch smile that she gave me was reassuring. Salma told her about the offer of the job. 'Will you stay?' she asked.

I waited for what seemed a long time, uncertain how openly I should speak. 'I don't think so,' I said.

Mariam nodded approvingly. I did not dare glance at Salma.

'Why not?' Salma asked. She did not sound distressed or disturbed, and I felt slightly hurt that she was not more upset. She just sounded interested.

'Because he wants to go and do things for himself first,' Mariam said. 'Why should he want to work in a butcher's shop or run endless errands for your father? He's got better things to do, haven't you? Find out about Picasso and Tolkien for a start!'

'I was just interested, Mariam,' Salma protested. 'Anyway, there are better things in life than finding out about Picasso and Tolkien.'

'Like what?' exclaimed Mariam, amazed by this heresy.

'Like learning to waltz,' said Salma, smiling at her friend. 'I've been teaching him how to waltz.'

'Hmmm! I see I'm behind the times here,' said Mariam. 'Are you taking him to a ball or something? Is there anything else you've taught him? I hope underneath all this new sophistication there's still the nice country boy that I met a few weeks ago.'

'You sound like two witches discussing a morsel that one of you is about to eat,' I protested.

'About to?' said Mariam, pretending to be surprised. 'I thought that the meal was all over ... '

'Mariam!' groaned Salma.

'Listen, Hassan,' said Mariam, talking with a cooing maternal voice. 'If they're nasty to you, come to me. There's always a home for you here.'

We went back to the Indian café for lunch, and Mariam was like somebody let out of prison. She talked endlessly,

147

teasing Salma and manufacturing stories about the other customers. She told us about her brother, who was expected back from America any day. He had married an American woman, and her parents, shocked and grief-stricken, were awaiting his return without any of the joy that they hoped to feel.

'Let that be a lesson to you,' she said to me. 'Don't complicate your parents' lives. In your wanderings around the globe, remember just to use the women that you find there. Don't bother to marry one. That's just dirty. I presume you will be wandering the globe?'

'How?' asked Salma. There was just a hint of plaintiveness in her voice, and my heart warmed at the sympathy.

'He'll find a way. Won't you, Picasso?'

We said goodbye in the street. Mariam made comical faces as she talked about returning to the dissertation. She told me I should go and see her on her own sometime.

It seemed that we walked for hours, only talking now and then: past parked cars and hotel doorways, past shops selling records of Jim Reeves and Elvis Presley, and everything else from shoe-laces to television sets. Past newsagents and magazine stands that sold pictures of Castro and Idi Amin. We saw old men lying drunk in the streets. We walked under green trees, past trinkets displayed on pavements, past fat nannies pushing prams. A man was forecasting the end of the world from the roof of a bus. A policeman stiffened to salute a passing minister's car. A motor cyclist thundered past, dangerously near the kerb. Finally we sat down on a park bench, within sight of the government buildings. We were shielded from the roads by flowering bushes and ornamental trees. She took my hand, raised it to her mouth and kissed it. We traded shy smiles. She released my hand, far too soon. I was too surprised to do anything.

'Why won't you stay?' she asked. She asked gently, not demanding but asking to understand.

'Because I don't want to be owned. I don't want to be dependent on how your father feels about me. I don't want to become like those managers who work for him. I'm not just being unkind about your father. That's how he's done things, and that's how he's succeeded. I don't think I'm the right person ... Do you understand? I haven't explained very well, but I don't mean to be unkind. I wish I could stay.'

She wanted me to say more, but I could not get the words out. I had no experience of scenes like these, and when I had tried the words out in my mind, they had sounded cloying and untrue. 'I wish I could stay,' I repeated.

'I wish you could stay too,' she said, smiling at my failure. 'But you don't have to go yet, do you?'

'No,' I replied. 'It's been ... wonderful meeting you. I'll miss you.'

'Perhaps you'll come back,' she said.

'I will.'

'You asked me something a while ago,' she said, leaning away from me. 'And I didn't answer you.'

'About your mother,' I said.

'She died when I was a child,' she went on. 'She poisoned herself.'

'Oh no.' I held her in my arms and felt her sigh and lean against me. After a moment she pushed herself off and sat up.

'I don't know why,' she said. 'Let me talk about it. My father never speaks of her. I used to ask him when I was younger. Oh, he told me things like she, came from Malindi ... and that ... God took her away when I was small ... that kind of thing. He has been very good, my father. I know he seems harsh and impatient, and he's irritable and sometimes cruel ... but he's been very good. He's a good man,' she said, her eyes beginning to water.

'Yes, I know,' I said.

'Ali and him. Ali has been with us for a long time. You must have wondered, the things he does ... He's almost one of the family. Well, I'm sure that's not how he sees it. He's still the servant.'

'How did you find out? About your mother?' I asked.

'Mariam found out. We've known each other since we were children. She was always like an elder sister. They kept it from her as well, all these years. It slipped out. Her mother told her. You know how secretive people are about these things. She said she couldn't get very much out of her mother. And I just don't know how to ask my father about it. It probably sounds spineless to you.'

'No,' I said. 'I know exactly what you mean.'

'My mother poisoned herself and I don't know how to ask about what had happened. I'm very afraid of hurting him more. I'm even more afraid that he won't tell me, and he'll turn away from me. He gets so angry sometimes. He goes into these rages ... '

'My mother warned me,' I said, smiling.

'Did she?' asked Salma, laughing. Tears were running down her face. 'It's not that I need to understand her more. I can't do anything about her. But to understand him ... and us ... between us. He's hiding this misery, and he won't even ... let me know about it. He's been like that all these years, and only last year I began to understand why. He won't let me ask him, and I feel I should.'

I took her hand and held it between both of mine.

'And now you're here to make everything even more complicated,' she said, reaching out and touching my face with her hand. She laughed. 'He told me you'd be coming.

150

We made such fun of you. He told me about your mother, when they were children. All the old days … '

'Did he tell you about my father?'

'Yes,' she said. 'He told me.'

'Did he tell you that he was in prison?'

'Yes,' she said. 'He told me everything.'

'Did he tell you that my father had buggered a little boy? And that the little boy had nearly gone mad? And that people say that he used to sell little boys to the Arabs? And that he's a drunk and spends as much time as he can in brothels?'

'Yes,' she said.

'God, what you must have expected!'

I felt suddenly very sorry for them, and for all the misery I had added to their lives. It must have seemed a terrible betrayal that their own child should think of them so unfeelingly.

'We expected a clown,' said Salma. 'We expected somebody we could laugh at. But you came.' She laughed and touched me again. 'Now he feels guilty. He shouldn't have asked you to come. He can't help you. You know that, don't you? He's had a very bad time. What you were saying about the managers … They've cheated him. All those managers are new. They all steal from him. He shouldn't have asked you to come. He knows that.'

'It doesn't matter,' I said. 'I knew as soon as I came here. You both made that clear.'

'I'm sorry,' she said, looking comically contrite.

'No, I was a clown when I first came. Not for the reasons you expected. All that biriani performance … I think I was doing all that for myself, being such a crass creep that I could pretend that I was not being serious, that I was superior to the begging mission I was on. Something like that … But I'm glad I came. I met you. And I'm glad in other ways that I came. I'm only sorry that I'll have to leave, and not see you.'

'But you'll be back.'

'Yes, I'll be back,' I said.

'What will you do?' she asked.

'I don't know. I'll go back home … and find some way …'

It was beginning to get dark when we decided to move. She suggested the cinema, reluctant as I was to return to the house. I was worried what Bwana Ahmed would do if we were late, but she did not seem anxious about that. 'When you go, you must write,' she said.

'I will,' I said. The streets were too brightly lit for me to embrace her. The cinema was showing *The Confessions of an English Opium Eater*. We decided that it was too dreary, but we were both desperate for the toilet. We were forced to buy tickets just for the pleasure of using the lavs. It was worth the money. There were carpets on the floor, air extractors humming gently overhead, subtle perfumes scenting the air.

I felt foolish holding hands on the bus, and our elbows seemed to get in the way. The bus was almost empty but we talked in whispers. In the end, casting caution to the winds, she rested her head on my shoulder and I put my arm around her. We arrived only too soon. As we strolled down the path she moved away from me. It must have been eight or nine in the evening, pitch dark everywhere, except for the squares of ground lit up by the light from the windows. I stood behind her as she struggled with the lock. The door was yanked out of her hands, and her father stood before us, a squat lump of rage.

'Where have you been?' he shouted through gritted teeth. 'Get in here.'

He motioned sharply for us to enter. As Salma walked past him, he cuffed her powerfully on the back of her head. She staggered forward then turned round to face him, her mouth open with shock and hurt. Tears formed in her eyes. He stepped forward and slapped her across the face. She staggered again, crying out with pain. 'How could you do this? After everything how could you do this?' he shouted.

He held his head and groaned. She shook her head, her eyes now streaming tears. 'Daddy,' she said, moving towards him. He looked up, then stepped forward to meet her and punched her full in the mouth. Her whole face leapt with surprise and fear. Blood spurted out of her mouth.

'Go to your room!' he screamed. 'Go!'

He turned away from the sight of her, rubbing his face with his hands to wipe away what he had seen. She stood where she was, sobbing while the blood ran from her mouth. He turned back to her. She clasped her hand over her mouth to silence the sobs. 'Go!' he pleaded.

He watched her hurry towards the living-room door, then turned to me. His face was vicious with hate. He raised a fist and shook it at me. He turned on his heels and walked to the living-room, calling over his shoulder, 'Come.'

'Sit down,' he said, pacing up and down by the windows. I ignored the instruction. He glared at me, swelled to the point of bursting and screamed, 'Sit down!'

I sat down. He resumed his pacing for a few minutes more. To hell with him, I thought, and stood up. He stopped in the middle of the room, his hands clasped behind his back.

'You're an animal,' he said, gritting his teeth as he tried to control himself.

My legs were trembling. I told myself that I was not really frightened, that I had been through this before, that

I was just primed to defend myself. Oh God, I thought, wait till they hear about this.

'What kind of a disgusting animal are you?' he shouted, shaking with rage. He resumed his pacing. Now and again he glanced at me, as if I was a slug that was crawling across his floor. At last he stopped, shook his head with bewildered anger. 'I was wrong, I will admit. I should not have asked you here. It was wrong of me. I tried my best. I welcomed you … like … like one of our own. I was wrong to ask you here, but I tried to … I offered you a job. I can't help you. I should not have asked you. Did you have to do this? Was this your way of paying us back for the way we treated you? I opened my house to you. I welcomed you. I welcomed you … and you take advantage. You abuse my daughter. You abuse my blood, my name. I watched you, and I should have stopped you. But I didn't think you were capable of this. Didn't they teach you anything? Didn't they teach you any manners where you came from? You stay in a man's house and then you abuse his daughter. Oh God, I've never learnt.'

I sensed that there would be no attempt at a beating. I would have to keep quiet and swallow his anger, and then perhaps attempt to explain. He glared at me as if daring me to speak. 'You're an animal,' he said, and took a deep breath to calm himself down. 'You're an animal! Why will I never learn? Please pack your things and get out. Now, please, now! I must go and see to my daughter.' Suddenly he began to shout again. 'Can't you think of anything else you'd like to do? Don't you want to get a knife and stab me as well? Oh get out of my house. Get out!' His fists were clenched by his side, his arms were shaking. His face was twisted with pain. I wanted to stop him, roughly shake him up and shove him against the wall. I wanted to tell him that because he felt pain did not mean that he understood what he had done, or that he had any right to beat people. That his petty bullying was creating more waste than should be in the power of one stupid man.

'I haven't done anything,' I started.

'I don't want to hear a word from you,' he shouted.

'And your daughter hasn't done anything.'

'Shut your mouth. Just pack your things and get out. Now! I don't want to hear any explanations or any apologies from you. I'll be getting in touch with your father. He'll know all about this. He'll be a very proud man when he hears from me.' He glared at me over a long silence. He did not need to say more but I knew he would. We both understood what he meant about my father. The son of such a man could not be expected to behave too differently.

'You hurt people for no reason,' I said. 'There is no need for any of this. There was no need to hit Salma.'

He growled and stepped forward. 'If you had not been my sister's son I would've killed you and faced the consequences.'

'Kill me. Don't let your sister stop you from doing what is right. There is not one thing about you that frightens me. I haven't dishonoured you. You've dishonoured yourself.'

'Aaah, go away,' he said, pushing me aside with a swipe of the hand. 'Go back to that criminal father of yours. He'll understand what you've done, the filthy man.' He spat on the floor and pushed me towards the door.

'Listen to me' I said, stopping and turning to face him. 'You're a stupid man, and I hope your God will forgive you for what you're doing. You can try to build a prison for your daughter, but I'll be back for her.'

He made no reply, standing there quite still, staring at me. My lower lip was trembling, and I prayed to God that

155

I would not burst into tears. He followed me as I walked down the corridor to the bedroom. Salma's door was shut, and I passed it without pausing. I gathered up my few things and rammed them into the bag. There was a note on the bed. I picked it up and put it in my pocket. Bwana Ahmed bin Khalifa was standing by the door, watching me. He pointed with his finger for me to go. He stayed with me all the time to prevent me seeing her. I walked past him, my neck tingling with anticipation of a blow. He followed me to the front door, and stood there until I had reached the road. No one ran after me, but the thought of the note gave me comfort.

I did not want to wait for a bus. I wanted to walk and think and mortify myself. I wanted to struggle on in the dark, hungry and tiring, chased by angry dogs. Perhaps I would have to sleep in the open, to be attacked by thugs and robbed and beaten. Two cars passed me, on each occasion accelerating to speed past. Something wailed in the distance, stretching out for long seconds in the night. With a gentle patter it began to rain. It quickly changed character, becoming hard, fast-falling drops of water that exploded in my face. What would Picasso have done? Would he have gone back? I felt in my pocket for the note. I stopped in the road and yelled out for more rain, feeling a desolate figure in the infinite landscape of the night. The rain beat down harder, approving this anguish, egging me on. Perhaps I could get a job in Nairobi, selling trinkets on the pavement. Perhaps Moses would take me on as a junior partner. Anything would be better than returning like this. I yelled out Salma's name in the night, wondering if it would make me feel worse. It did, so I yelled it again, with more feeling.

There was no choice but to go back to my people. And when I returned to them, they would tell me of their ancestors, God's chosen race, on whom rain had beaten down in their wanderings, cruel wayfarers deplenishing the land. They would tell me of their ancestral glories, their kingdoms and their conquests. I had come back empty-handed when I could have returned with columns in stocks. I had come back with nothing when they had returned with ivory and aphrodisiac horns. What little could be done I had failed to do.

No one asked what happened to the women they left behind in their parched peninsula, these people of the chosen race. No doubt they languished in their grim certitudes, knowing that God had given them the black pagan to enslave and make their husbands prosperous. They made sons on watering days, when their husbands came back with tales and booty from the black lands. For years on end they ate salads with the goats, left behind to scratch life from barren rock and dust, dressed in mourning black rags, calling to their children with shrill cries of warning. God's people had sprung from that barren rock and dust to save the world from a heresy. They sent their grown sons to us, to ravish and herd us in blood. Of my own line, there are merely salt-sellers, sailors and masseurs, with a reluctantly acknowledged share of black blood in their veins. Glory, glory, there was not even a painter who carried our name.

A car stopped in the rain, its engine throbbing beside me. A European sat behind the wheel. He motioned for me to jump in but I shook my head and waved him on. I had heard enough about the perversions people were offered by kindly Europeans who had stopped to give them a lift. He shrugged, raised a hand in farewell and drove off.

I searched for the note. The rain had now become a nuisance. The darkness was denying me word from my beloved. Beloved! After so much talk of death and pain! I would have to learn from nothing the words I had never said. I saw a light in the distance, such a long way away. It was suddenly important to read the note. I ran in the rain, yelling back at the yard dogs that barked at my passage. A police car drew up alongside me as I reached the light. I stopped to watch, old fears rising.

'I'm just going to the railway station,' I volunteered, lifting up my bag as evidence. As I held it up to the light, it resembled nothing so much as a burglar's kit of tools. The policemen did not seem to be interested. 'We're not going that way,' one of them said. They exchanged a few words and drove off, afraid that I would ask them for a lift.

I opened the note carefully, lest in my excitement I should crush the soggy folds into pulp. She had scrawled: *Don't forget to write. S.* Underneath that she had written Mariam's full name and her University address. Was that all? No passionate words of promise? No blood-stained vows? Still, it was enough, my poor wounded Salma. I had not lost her. I threw the note in a puddle under the lamp-post. It suited the drama of the moment. I looked for a landmark so I could remember the place. I made it a shrine, to return to on a pilgrimage when I came back to claim her. I picked up my bag and strolled towards the lights of the city.

I arrived at the station in the middle of the night. The gates were shut but passengers for the early morning train to Jinja and Kampala were sleeping in the yard. They told me that the coast train left in the early evening. I stretched out to sleep on the comfortless ground, but the two men who had told me about the train started to bother me. They wanted money first, but then they just became threatening. I left them and moved nearer the gates where there were more people. I found space near a family and tried to sleep.

As soon as it was light enough, I left to find the University. I waited at the University gates until I saw people moving around. Mariam was still in bed when I knocked on her door. She opened the door a fraction and peeped out.

'What's happened?' she asked, squeezing her eyes to press the sleep out. 'I only went to bed an hour ago.'

'I'm sorry,' I said. 'I just wanted to talk to you. I'll come back later.'

'Is something wrong?' she asked, suddenly attentive.

'I've been thrown out,' I said, smiling at my own absurdity.

'Oh God,' she groaned. 'Give me a few minutes.'

We went to the café for breakfast, and I told her what had happened. 'That stupid man,' she said. 'You don't know what that man has done. I daren't even tell Salma. You write to me and I'll pass the letters on. Don't let him frighten you.'

'What do you mean? What has he done?'

She told me about Salma's mother and what happened to her. She was reluctant to speak at first, but the more she said the more involved she became in her own story. 'A friend of theirs, I don't know his name, was staying with them. He came from Uganda too. They knew each other as children. Something went wrong, his business had failed or something. I think he may even have had to go to prison. Anyway, they took him in. He lived with them for months. Then Uncle Ahmed found out that they were sleeping together. Well, he said they were sleeping together. He went into a rage and fought this friend. I think he hurt him very badly, a knife or something. Then he locked Salma's mother in a room. People knew about it because the friend told everybody and insisted on his innocence. Ami Ahmed never went out. He didn't even go to work. He just stayed at

159

home, standing guard over his wife. My mother told me that some people tried to go and see him, to talk him out of his madness, but he refused to see anyone. Somebody saw Salma's mother at a window. She looked like a mad woman, filthy hair and rags. In the end the police came and took her to hospital. By the time they let her out, Uncle Ahmed had calmed down, but it was too late for her. She was terrified of everything. He would not let her go anywhere on her own. In the end she poisoned herself. I think she was already mad by then. Mother said they had to have a keeper for her, like a lunatic. She saw her once, soon before she died. It was Idd, and my mother and father had gone to greet the family. Mother had to go to the toilet, and while she was in there she heard somebody outside the door. When she came out she saw it was Salma's mother. She said she looked a little neglected but did not seem unhappy. You know how we keep mad relatives locked up in our houses, and she just assumed that Salma's mother had become one of them. Then she poisoned herself. I didn't know any of this, until my mother told me. I didn't know how to tell Salma, but someone will have to. He won't do it. I think he'll kill himself one of these days.'

'Why do you say that?' I asked.

'I'm just saying it,' she said. 'I don't know anything. But he can't live with that. One day Salma will find out, and then he won't be able to bear the way she'll see him. He lives for her now. He's been trying to make amends through her. One day she'll find out. And now he hits her. How that stupid man must be hurting.'

'I'm sorry. I didn't know ... I think I've made things worse,' I said.

'No you didn't,' she said, smiling. 'But you're very fortunate to get away with your life. You're a lucky man,

160

Picasso. It was a good thing you happened to her. I don't know why yet, but I think it is. She'll have to know. They'll have to sort it out.'

'Will you tell her?'

She shook her head. 'I don't know,' she said. 'I'll go and see her tomorrow, talk to her. I'll tell her I saw you.'

'Tell her I'll write,' I said.

'Is that the best you can do? I'm sure Picasso would've thought of a more interesting message than that. Never mind, I'll make it up,' she said.

She took me back to her room. I tried to sleep while she went to the library to work. Later in the afternoon she came with me to the station to see me off. She barged confidently through the crowds and came all the way into the train with me. She helped me find a free bunk and sat with me while we waited for the time of departure.

'What will you do now?' she asked.

'I don't know,' I said. 'Everything seems so difficult. I have to go and explain all this to my parents for a start. I know how they'll take it. Then I'll have to sort something out for myself. Perhaps I'll get a job in the Post Office or in the docks … '

She slapped me on the thigh. 'Stop feeling sorry for yourself,' she said. 'Go back there, young Picasso, and tell them what needs to be told. Then go and conquer the world. Only don't forget to write.'

She kissed me on the cheek when it was time to go. She stood on the platform waving the train away, plump and plain and full of courage, grinning at the discovery of a new friend.

5

She grinned when she looked up and saw me standing in front of her in the yard. She made to get up and I bent down and kissed her on the top of her head. She said my name as if remonstrating with me, but with pleased surprise. When she looked again at me her eyes were wide with enquiry.

'I'm back,' I said, throwing my arms open.

'I can see that,' she said, and waited momentarily for me to continue. She did not ask any questions. She knew that my news could not be good. She bustled to get me some food and warm some water for a wash. She did not seem as tired as I remembered her, and she smiled as she rebuked me for not warning her of my return.

'I left in a hurry,' I said, unable to suppress a smile.

'What happened?' she asked, wiping her hands on her dress as she came nearer. She peered at me while I tried to look unconcerned. 'Why did you leave in a hurry?'

'I'll tell you,' I said. 'I'll tell you everything.'

'Yes, you have a wash and have something to eat first,' she said quickly, rebuking herself for rushing me. 'Then we can talk. Are you well? Are you feeling well?'

'Headache,' I said, touching my head. 'It's the train. All that noise.'

She smiled and then reached to touch me on the temple as if afraid to hurt me. Saida appeared at the back door, rubbing sleep from her eyes.

'Oh it's you,' she said. 'You're back.'

'And it's nice to see you too,' I said, lunging for her. She squealed with fright and jumped back into the house.

'Don't make so much noise,' my mother said, dropping her voice to a whisper. 'Bi Mkubwa is ill. She fell out of bed and hurt herself. She won't go to hospital. She says she wants that Indian doctor to come. Do you remember him? Dr Mehta. I told her he's dead, but she still won't go to the hospital. She says she's all right, but she's not. She groans all night.'

'Sorry,' I said. 'Is Ba at home?'

'No,' she said.

'Zakiya?'

She made a noise between a groan and a grunt. 'I don't know what we're going to do about her. She won't listen to me any more. Perhaps you can talk to her. Some nights she doesn't come home at all. I don't know what we can do,' she said in a voice that seemed on the verge of breaking on every word. 'She became worse when you left. You talk to her. Perhaps you can make her see some sense.'

'I will,' I said. 'I'll talk to her. Don't make yourself miserable. She's not a child any more.'

'How can you say that!' she cried. 'She's like somebody who's gone mad.'

'Mama, I didn't mean that it doesn't hurt. Only that if she's determined to destroy herself, then we can't talk her out of it.'

'I won't listen to that,' she said. She bristled at me with a look of such bitterness that I wished I could take my words back. She closed her eyes and sighed. 'I'm sorry, this is not the way to greet you back. But we must not give her up like that.'

'We won't,' I said. 'I'll talk to her … '

'Yes,' she said urgently, keen to put the subject to one side. 'Go and wash, now. I'll get your room ready and then we can talk.'

'What room?' I asked. 'Since when have I had a room?'

'Well, you're a big man now,' she said, grinning. 'And I'm getting tired of coming out in the morning to see you lying there with your *kikoi* open and your things dangling all over the place. So you can have the little guest-room.'

'Well, that's an honour.'

'Don't be cheeky,' she said, slapping me on the arm. 'Go and wash. Go on, my father, and I'll get your food ready.'

The bathroom recalled with pungent force the comforts I had left behind. It did not take much effort to pinch my nose and close my eyes to the squalor, and think of the warmth of my welcome. When I came out, I saw that my mother had spread a new mat in the yard, a *busati*. Saida was already stretched out on it, dozing. She stirred as I sat down beside her.

'She said she wanted to wait and greet you properly,' my mother said. 'She should be in bed. Bi Mkubwa is groaning again. The poor little one finds it difficult when she's like that, but your grandmother insists that she stays in there. She says she gets frightened on her own.'

Saida sat up with her eyes still closed. My mother took her by the hand and smartly yanked her to her feet. Saida whimpered in protest and turned back to me. 'Have you got a present for me?' she asked.

'For an ugly thing like you? No, of course not,' I said.

She made a face of indescribable ugliness as she was being dragged away. My mother came back out looking harassed and unhappy. 'She's groaning again. It's not right for a child to have to sleep with her,' she said in a whisper.

'Then don't let her. If she's as ill as you say, suppose something happens. Suppose she ... '

'Don't say it,' she interrupted me. 'I'll have to go and sleep with her. Saida can sleep in our room.'

She dropped her eyes as I looked at her. I was thinking of the time when I had been accorded that honour. 'Let her come and sleep in with me,' I said. 'We can move a mattress or a bedspread in tomorrow.'

'All right,' she said in a small voice, assuming that I was blaming her for past wrongs. 'You haven't had a very cheerful homecoming.'

'I've had a wonderful homecoming. I'm very glad to be back.'

'Was it very difficult in Nairobi? You didn't get into any trouble, did you? No wait, let me just get the food,' she said. She made me an onion omelette, and brought me three slices of *boflo*. 'We don't have any milk. Do you mind dry tea or shall I make you some coffee?' she asked.

'Dry tea will be nice,' I said. 'Can you put some ginger in it? Do we have any?'

'Dry tea and ginger! Is this what the Europeans in Nairobi drink?' she asked.

'No,' I said. 'They drink coffee with milk and sugar in it. You should try it. It's what civilised people drink.'

She knew that things had gone wrong. She was making it clear to me whose side she was on, trying to make me feel better about talking. 'How's Ba?' I asked when she came to sit with me.

'He's the same,' she said, turning her mouth down in that familiar gesture of long-suffering resignation. 'He still thinks he's a young man. You know how he is. Perhaps he's a little worse, I don't know.'

'What do you mean?' I asked. 'How worse?'

'You know how he is,' she said, rubbing her temples with the tips of her fingers. 'He drinks too much and then swears that he'll get better and that he'll stop … He means it, and he weeps and swears … ' She stopped and stared at me,

166

surprised at how much she had told me. She nodded and continued. 'He's going through one of his times. He didn't come home last night. When he comes he's so drunk … They'll sack him from his job, and then God knows what we'll do. He goes out like this and does all these dirty things. He thinks I don't know.'

She looked at me silently for a long time, her eyes large with an old pain. Then a faint smile started to appear on her face. 'That's your strength,' she said, her smile growing. 'You hold steady with your silence. You don't let it weaken. At the back of it I can hear the small little noise of your heart beating. And it's only when you were not here that I knew I had heard it all the time. Do you understand what I mean? You hold steady while we tire and weaken, and all the time your heart remains true. What a homecoming you've had! I wanted to say that, and to thank God that He has brought you safely back to us.'

I ate in silence, struggling to hold back the tears that threatened to destroy my new image as a strong, silent man.

She had shut the window of the guest-room and sprayed it with insect-killer. The smell of the DDT mingled with the smell of dust and new whitewash to produce a rasping atmosphere that seemed to be tearing the lining off the back of my throat. She had gone to check on my grandmother, saying that she would not be long. When she came in, she sat in the chair next to me. The room was so small that we were sitting barely inches apart. She sighed, and gathered the kanga tightly round her shoulders, expecting not to find any pleasure in what she was about to hear.

'I'm ready,' she said.

'He did not intend to help me,' I said. 'He had decided even before I went. He told me himself later, but I knew it anyway as soon as I arrived there. They thought I would be a clown and they would have a laugh at my expense. Don't look like that, mama. That's true. Even the servant treated me like a … beggar when I first went there. So I decided I would at least have a holiday.'

'He told you himself that he had never intended to help you?' she asked. I knew she believed me, and I don't think she was really surprised. 'Did you remind him about the inheritance?'

'He would've liked that,' I said. 'Then he really would have had something to laugh at me about. You don't know how they live. He convinces himself that he's right about everything. He thinks everybody wants to cheat him. He offered me a job. He asked me to stay and work for him, but I didn't want that kind of life … bustling around doing nothing, and suspicion all the time.'

'But you should have, you should have mentioned the inheritance,' she insisted.

'I couldn't. He was treating me like some poor relation from the sticks who'd come to ask a favour. If I'd started to demand your inheritance he'd have assumed I was being presumptuous and kicked me out of his house sooner than he did.'

'He kicked you out?' she asked, suddenly looking angry. 'That Ahmed with the big mouth! He was always like that, always big big big man, even when we were children. How dare he?'

'You didn't tell me he had a daughter,' I said, trying not to smile but failing.

I saw her anger deflating. Her jaw slackened and her mouth fell ostentatiously open. 'What did you do?' she asked.

'I like her. I'm going to marry her one day.'

'Oh my God. Couldn't you just do what you had gone there for? Couldn't you just leave that alone? What did you do? What did you do to her?' she demanded, getting angry with me.

'I didn't do anything. He thought I did, that's why he threw me out.'

'Your family is cursed,' she said, panting now with anger. 'You couldn't leave that alone for a few days? You had to go there and behave like a ram when you know what he thinks of us. I would've thrown you out too if you'd come and done that. Don't you have any respect for yourselves, any of you? You're all the same, just like your father, all of you. Then you pretend that he had already decided not to help you.'

'I'm not pretending. It's true. He really was not going to help,' I said. 'And she's beautiful. Her name is Salma, and she likes me too. Her eyes are grey, and her face is … a little round, and cheerful. She speaks softly and is always kind. She is very thoughtful and clever. And one day I'm going to marry her.'

'You went there to ask for help, so that you could do something useful with your life. You didn't go there to play Prince Qamar Zaman, and dishonour your uncle's daughter.'

'I did not dishonour anybody,' I said, speaking calmly and smiling at her. I wanted to convince her about Salma, to show her that things were not as they seemed. 'Nothing happened. We just went to town together a few times, and we talked. If it wasn't for her, I would've been treated like a dog in that house. She argued with her father, persuaded him that what they had done was wrong. You wait until you meet her. You'll like her, mama.'

'All right, she's wonderful,' she said, raising her hand to stop me. 'But it wasn't right what you did. To go into somebody's house as a guest and do something like that. You were wrong to do that.'

'I know,' I said. 'I told myself every day. I went this way and that way ... but I was afraid that if I left I would never see her again.'

'And nothing happened?' she asked.

'Nothing happened. Except that I told her ... and I know that she loves me too.'

'How do you know?' she asked, as if suspicious that I was making too much of what I knew of her.

'She embraced me. And she asked me to write.'

'To write! Don't write. Your uncle might find the letters,' she said.

'It doesn't matter,' I said. 'I told him I was going back for her one day.'

She chuckled, and then laughed. 'You must be serious,' she said. 'What did he say?'

I had hoped that she would not be able to resist the thought of a girl I had found to love. I told her of what happened when we came back from Nairobi that night. I did not tell her the things that Bwana Ahmed said about Ba.

'Did you know about her mother?' I asked.

'Yes,' she said after a pause. 'I knew that she died badly.'

'She poisoned herself,' I said.

'Yes,' she said.

'Salma doesn't know why, but other people do.'

'Because of the man?' she asked.

'Because of what he did to her afterwards. And perhaps it wasn't true about the man anyway.'

'It must have been,' she cried.

'Like it's true about Ba? People have been saying that too.'

She winced a little, and then nodded to show that she understood what I meant. 'Perhaps it isn't true about the man,' she said. 'I knew her as a child. She came from a very rich family in Jinja.'

'That's why he was so angry. He thought I had done the same thing as this man, come into his house and dishonoured him. Salma doesn't know. He hasn't told her. He won't even talk about her mother. She's known that something is wrong, but he won't say anything. She found out what little she knows from somebody else. Why are parents like that? You wouldn't tell me about Ba either. I thought it was something I was, something I did to you, that made you that way to me. And all the time the two of you were going through the misery of all that talk.'

'Don't start that again,' she pleaded with her eyes shut.

'I'm not starting that again. I'm just sorry for all the misery I added to your lives. Because I didn't know, and I didn't think.'

She started to cry. 'Leave it now. Leave it,' she said. 'Tell me more about your beloved. What is she doing? Is she working? Does she speak our language or does she only talk in English?'

'Of course she speaks our language. She likes ice-cream,' I said.

'We can get ice-cream here,' she said.

We talked late into the night. Now and then she went to check on Bi Mkubwa, and then I would find myself dozing with tiredness. On each occasion I roused myself in time, so that she should not see how tired I was. I knew she was waiting up for Zakiya and my father, and I did not want her to be alone with those worries and with all the additional ones I had given her. She began to take heart as her anger with Bwana Ahmed increased. She was quite pleased, she said, that I had turned down his offer of a job. 'It's God's judgment on him. He denies you a little money which is your right anyway, and God takes his daughter away from him.'

'Don't exaggerate,' I said.

'It serves him right.'

'I haven't taken his daughter away from him yet. I have to find a way of making a fortune first. By that time I might be an old man, and she might have married somebody else.'

'Don't be silly,' she said. 'Something will turn up.'

'Especially if God is on our side on this one.'

'Don't blaspheme,' she said, her eyes flashing at me.

In the end we both got too tired, and we sat dozing in our chairs. 'It's very late, past midnight. They won't be coming home tonight,' I said. 'I'll go and lock up.'

'No,' she said sharply. 'You go to sleep ... I ... I'll lock up.'

I knew she was lying, that she would go and sleep outside in the yard as she had been doing for years, and wait until they both turned up before locking the doors.

'I must talk to Ba tomorrow ... about all this. He'll be getting a letter from Uncle Ahmed,' I said.

'I'll do it,' she said.

'I'm not afraid,' I protested.

'I wasn't thinking of you,' she said. 'I was thinking of him. Let me do it.'

Neither of them came home that night. They both turned up in the mid-morning of the next day. They had heard from other people that I was back. My father looked worn out, and I could see that his eyes were hurting with lack of sleep. He greeted me heartily, as if nothing was the matter, and I had only just arrived. I asked after his health and he replied at length, too preoccupied with dissembling the shame he felt to enquire after my adventures. My mother took him away before he had the chance to recover. I heard his oaths and his anger, and then I heard him laugh. I thought my father would appreciate the poaching of the rich miser's daughter. When he came out he was trying not to grin. He made as if to pass me by, and then turned suddenly and slapped me on the shoulders.

'So that's what we paid the fare for,' he said, laughing. 'So you can go and seduce respectable people's daughters. It was wrong what you did.' He dropped his voice, 'But it served the fucking miser right. He thinks he's too good for us, but you showed him.'

'Ba,' I said, trying to interrupt him.

'That's two women he's lost now, that stupid penis. One maybe you can understand, it's bad luck, a tragedy ... but two. What kind of a fuckhead is he? He invites you all the way up there just to make a joke!'

'Ba,' I said, putting my hand on his arm. 'Bi Mkubwa is very ill. She was very bad last night. We must take her to hospital.'

'She won't go,' he said softly, squeezing his eyes to ease the pain. 'I've tried but she won't go.'

'We must try again,' I said, lowering my voice. 'She might be dying.'

He looked as if he would stop me, and then nodded. He looked old and very tired. He nodded again and looked away from me. 'We must take her today,' I said. 'Tell her whatever you want, but we must persuade her to go to the hospital.'

'All right,' he snapped. 'I'll go to her now.'

Zakiya came while he was with her. She came to look for me in my room, dressed to kill. She stood leaning against the door, looking casual and sophisticated.

'I hear you're getting married,' she said, mocking my innocence.

I stood up and went to her. She lifted herself from the door, looking frightened. I put my hands on her shoulders

173

and squeezed them. 'What are you doing? What's happening to you?' I asked.

Her face puckered like a child's and she began to cry. I pulled her into the room and held her while she sobbed. She clung to me, pressing her face into my shoulder. I felt the tears and saliva soaking through my shirt. When she had calmed down a little, she disengaged herself and left without saying a word. I called to her but she did not return. I ran after her but my father called me back, to say that Bi Mkubwa would go. I said I would go and call a taxi. I looked for Zakiya but I had lost her.

My father and I carried Bi Mkubwa to the car. I had not seen her since coming back. She looked drawn and very old. Her eyes were shut and she was panting for breath. My mother tried to clean her before we took her out, but she had the unmistakable smell of death, the smell of old faeces and urine. We sat on either side of her, supporting her when she rolled over. She mumbled and wept, and neither of us comforted her.

They turned us away at first, insisting that we join the long queues of the waiting sick. My father raged at the nurse while the crowds watched us. A woman warned the nurse that if the old lady died, her death would be on his head. The nurse looked frightened for a moment and then became very angry. He abused the woman so viciously that the crowd turned against him. Assailed from all sides, he went to call the charge nurse, who admitted Bi Mkubwa at once.

I stayed behind while my father went back to work. I followed the trolley to the ward, and waited while patients were rearranged to make room for my grandmother. The ward was like a vision of Hell. The walls were covered with grime. Windows faced the door of the ward, and all the window shutters had fallen off. The beds were crowded in, separated from each other by narrow alleyways, which were cluttered with pots and bags. Lines of string criss-crossed the room, from some of which hung mosquito nets. The ward smelt of pus and rotting bodies, and old vomit and dirty laundry, and every combination of the most vile stenches. Sick bodies sprawled on the metal beds. Some were leaning up to watch while most lay abandoned.

The nurses forced one of the women to get out of her bed. She was a thin and shrivelled old woman, and she complied without protest. She gathered her torn bits of bedding and dragged herself wearily towards the door. Her hands and feet were twisted and knotted with rheumatism. Her neck was bent as if she was carrying a burden, her shrunken head pointing at the ground like the beak of a scavenger. The nurses made a face at the bed she had vacated. The bare mattress was marked with stains and streaks of slime. They turned the mattress over and put my grandmother on it.

I asked them when the doctor would come but they said they did not know. They told me I could stay and wait if I wanted. I asked them what would happen to the old woman they had removed from the bed. The two nurses glanced at each other.

'Shall we bring her back then?' one of them asked me.

I waited on the veranda. The rheumatic old woman had joined other patients there. The doctor came late in the afternoon. He examined my grandmother and said that he would arrange for her to be X-rayed when he came back. He explained that he was going away to Denmark for a few days, as personal physician to the Minister of Culture, who was going there to order a statue of the leader. I asked if his assistant could not have the X-rays done. He told me he had no assistant.

We took turns to watch her. My father relieved me late in the afternoon, and my mother spent the night at the hospital. She died the following day, while I was asleep on the veranda. It was the nurses who came to tell me. They asked me to remove the body because they needed the bed. I asked for a stretcher but they said they had none. I said I would have to go for help and a bier. They put Bi Mkubwa's body in the sluice room at the end of the ward. There was no doctor to sign a death certificate. Without one we would not be able to bury her. I went for my father and he paid one of the nurses to sign the certificate. We took the body home in the back of a taxi, covered with old blankets.

I went to register her death at the Court, and obtained the chit to take to the cemetery. The grave-digger complained and I had to bribe him. We screened-off the yard and washed her body in the open, squeezing whatever would come out of her before embalming her with lavender. Zakiya came to help my mother prepare the house for visitors.

We buried her the next day. It was a sorry funeral-train that took her body to the cemetery, no more than half a dozen of us taking turns to carry her body to rest. My mother was the only one who cried, and she wept for the misery of those final years.

Life must go on, my father said and very soon resumed his old life. He did so with more discretion than before and with much less zest. The fire was dying out in him, and now he slipped in and out of the house, morose and apologetic. He never spoke to Zakiya.

She refused to listen to my entreaties. She told me of a room she had rented. She intended to move there at the end of the month. She did not need to spell out what the room would be used for. She told me about her boy-friend who would support her.

'He has his own family. He will use you until he tires of you, and then pass you on to somebody else. Please be sensible,' I pleaded.

'I can look after myself,' she said.

'That room will end up being a brothel,' I said, meaning to hurt her.

'Thank you,' she said with a bitter smile. 'You can come and see me there if you want. Unless that will shame you too much.'

'Of course I'll come. But why do you have to do this? Why do you have to live like this?'

'I don't know,' she screamed. 'I don't know. I don't know.'

When my mother found out, she begged her not to go. She knelt in front of Zakiya, pleading with her while tears trailed down her face. I forced my mother away in the end, dragging her in my arms while she sobbed and wailed. Zakiya did not leave then, but I knew it would only be a matter of time. She saw herself in a way I could not fully understand. She played her role to the full, dressing the part and swinging her hips with all the abandon of a hardened young prostitute. Yet she was ashamed of what she had become. It tore my heart to shreds just to watch her as she strutted through the streets.

I told my mother that I would not go. That was on the day that the government finally released our results. I had done even better than I expected, well enough for direct entry into the University. We did not have the fees, and a government scholarship was as much out of the question as it had ever been.

'There's enough to do here,' I said. She had taken to coming to my room every night and sitting with me. She did not say anything at first but looked at me with the old suspicion. I could not help laughing.

'There's nothing for you to do here,' she said sharply. 'What will you do in this place? Become like us?'

'I am like you,' I said. 'I'll go to the teachers' college. I'll become a teacher. They'll take me there, and you don't have to pay fees. I can still live at home if Ba will not object.'

'No, no,' she said with a look of pain. 'Go and do the things you want. Go away and do things, and live your life. Don't stay here. We can look after ourselves. And don't forget what you said about Salma, and how you said you will do all these things and come back for her. Don't stay just for us. This place will kill you.'

I applied to the college and they accepted me almost at once. I was to start at the beginning of the next academic year, in January. Zakiya told me I was a fool, and my mother shook her head over me. 'Who needs you here?' she asked.

'You need me,' I said, grinning at the derision and contempt with which she asked her question. 'You need my quiet strength.'

'We've survived without it so far. You just leave us to struggle on. We don't want your sacrifice.' She slapped me on the arm to stop me smiling. 'Do you hear? I'm not joking with you. Go and see what there is out there. Nobody needs you here. Who needs a teacher when we don't even have enough schools for our children?'

'What's wrong with being a teacher? They'll build the schools, and there's always need for teachers.'

'You're not listening,' she said, getting angry. 'What will they teach you in this college? How to bully little children? Is that what you want?'

'I don't have to bully the children. Not all teachers do that. I could be useful, and I would be here ... among my own people.'

She came back to the subject again and again, and Zakiya was always her willing ally. They never talked about this in front of my father. He seemed pleased that I would be staying, making jokes about using the stick on my future girl students.

'What about Salma?' my mother asked.

'Yes, what about your betrothed?' Zakiya asked.

'What betrothed? How am I going to convince her father that I'm anything but contemptible? Perhaps it was nothing more than the excitement of being in Nairobi. Perhaps it was just a holiday romance.'

'You *are* contemptible,' Zakiya said.

'Watch how you talk to your elder brother,' my mother warned. 'He could beat you with his stick.'

I had not expected them to be so insistent. It flattered me that they should care about what I would do, but it made it difficult to avoid the truth.

'You're just afraid,' Zakiya said. She had just moved to her rented room and this was the first time I visited her. 'All these years you've been talking about leaving, and now you don't have the nerve.'

'I don't have the money.'

'You're just afraid,' she said, shaking her head.

'All right, I am afraid,' I admitted. 'I've always been afraid. I find the thought of travelling to another place about which I know nothing, and where I know nobody, terrifying. I always have found it terrifying. But in any case, I don't even have the fare. What is the point of fretting about leaving when I don't even have the money for the fare? What is it out there that is worth such risks?'

'What has always been out there. It is still there, but you won't find out sitting on your backside in this dumb place.'

I took to wandering my old haunts, and I began to feel the return of the old hopelessness. My trip to Nairobi began to seem like a distant memory. The letter to Salma constantly defeated me. I slept late into the morning and wandered the streets in the heat of the day. The discomfort of the sun was like a penance for the useless hours spent in bed. I spent hours watching flies crawling over my body, watching them suck the sweat from my arms and legs.

I went to the docks almost every day. Now I was no longer a child the Customs guards did not stop me at the gate as they used to. There were always others strolling the wharves, gazing into the sea. There was a kiosk opposite the disembarkation building where the strollers stopped for a cold drink or a cup of tea. The man who ran the kiosk knew my father, had known him from the days when he used to work in the docks, filling in forms for people who could not write. He was very friendly and loved talking about his days at sea. He told me about his son who had stowed away in a ship from Mombasa to Glasgow where he now lived. I knew the story, and stories of people who had been found and thrown overboard. He laughed when I told him that. 'We found a stowaway on one ship I was on, and the captain made us throw him into the propellers. He was an Italian captain, out of Barawa. Another time we had this Afrikanda. We chased him all over the ship, and in the end he jumped overboard. We saw the sharks get him there in front of us.'

Some nights I dreamt of a crow I had seen as a child. Its claws had been cut off, and whenever it tried to land it landed on the raw stump of its legs. It blundered from tree to tree around the edge of our school playing-fields, pursued by a crowd of children hurling stones. Its end came as it flew across the fields towards the school buildings. It fell to the ground, its neck already limp with death. I dreamt that someone hid the crow under my pillow.

The first night I tried to sleep with the light on, my mother came into the room. She sat at the foot of the bed and waited for me to stop pretending that I was asleep. 'Shall I switch the light off? Or are you becoming afraid of the dark too?'

'Is Ba home?' I asked.

'Yes, he's drunk,' she said. 'Somebody beat him tonight. He's very quiet. I don't know how that man will end up.'

'I want to leave,' I said. 'I don't know how … '

She waited for me to continue.

'Ma, can't you say something?'

'What do you want me to say? You tell me how I can help you and I will. If you just want to talk, then I'm tired. One beaten man in this house is enough.'

'I want to try and get work on a ship,' I said. 'Ba will know some people … He might be able to speak to somebody. He might know somebody from the docks, from when he worked there. He might ask somebody for me.'

'Yes,' she said, smiling sadly. 'I'll tell him.'

6

SS *Alice*

29 October 1968

Dear Salma,

It has taken me a long time to get to this, and now that I'm here I am no longer sure that this is the right beginning. This is the seventh start I have made now, each one worse than the last. Seven is a propitious number, so I know this effort will turn out well despite its poor beginning.

It's three months now since I last saw you, since I left Nairobi in a blaze of glory. I expect that by now you are a student, and hardly have time to recall my flying visit to your railway-depot of a city. (That is not to be taken seriously: I expect you to recall every moment.)

I saw Mariam the day after I left you, and spoke with her at length. I already feel she is a good friend. She told me a lot about you. She promised that she would come and see you the next day, and I hope she did and brought you my love. I think of you every day. I promised I would write, and I intended to do so as soon as I got home. But I was a little overcome by events when I first arrived back. After that I just lost my nerve, although I could find a less painful way of describing it if I really tried. You were part of a vision of a fulfilled future, but I found so much misery here that I felt self-indulgent whenever I contemplated it. How could I even think about departure at such times? I thought of writing to greet you, just to make sure that you would not forget me, but even that seemed like a betrayal, like a kind of selfishness. How could I think like that? I don't know. Perhaps because I saw nothing but the misery and defeat of my people. I saw nothing but a pointless clinging to old habits. My grandmother died and we hardly mourned her. It was as if she had not lived with us, but had come like a visitor and had now gone on with her journey. I sensed our resignation, and started to feel the beginnings of an old hopelessness overtaking me. I felt that I should stay and be of use. I could not write to you feeling like that.

Perhaps I should have stayed. I intended to, but I am now three weeks away from home, between Bombay and Madras. I am working on a ship, SS *Alice*, as a medical orderly. I could not resist the opportunity, and often I feel that I have run away.

We left Bombay this morning, thank God. It's a nightmare city, crowded and noisy, full of the most incredible filth. Everyone seemed to be shouting or hustling, or begging. I must confess that I hardly left the port. The place frightened me. It is now late evening, and I am writing this on the top deck, under the lifeboat lights. We took on many passengers at Bombay, mostly bound for Singapore. Our cargo holds are full and will have no more capacity until we reach Singapore. Our stop at Madras is for the benefit of a few passengers who embarked at Mombasa.

This is a very dirty ship, adapted to carrying dirty wog passengers. One of its decks has been converted into a huge, dark barn, with endless rows of metal bunks hardly a yard apart. The bunks have no bedding on them, and some of the passengers sleep on the bare springs. They live and cook down there, spreading their bundles in the aisles, and lighting little Primus stoves to cook their rice and beans. It's a grim place, always dark, even when the few light bulbs are on. It smells of copra and damp jute, as if at one time it had been used as a hold. Underneath this, you can smell and taste human squalor, and hear echoes of the groans of the Middle Passage. There are always people sprawled on the bunks. Plump matrons swathed in old saris who look bloated and damp like creatures out of their element. Thin, wiry men whose eyes gaze into the half-light with the dreamy abandon of despair. Children who squeeze themselves into small foetal shapes, and lie like sick lambs waiting for death. We go among them with our pails and sponges and talk to them about hygiene.

My boss is called Dr Martin. He is an Australian and very wild. He does not take notice of anybody, but likes to think of himself as kind. He drinks a lot, and talks of the passengers as if they were mystics. He treats the crew as if they were pigs. He is trying to convince me that I'm too intelligent to be one of them. I was suspicious of him at first. I wasn't sure what he wanted. Now I think he means to be kind. He's shown me a picture of his girl-friend, who is waiting for him in Sydney. She's very good-looking.

I wish things were different. I wish I wasn't so far away. He is right to treat the crew as if they were pigs. They call me Jerk, meaning that is what I do with myself. Sometimes they call me Wog or Nigger. They are all so conscious of being men, and all want to be thought of as hard. The Greeks are the worst of all. *Chibuk, chibuk*, as if that is all they do when they are not chewing vine leaves and raping demi-goddesses.

I won't be back until the New Year, so I'll keep writing to you even though you can't reply. Perhaps when I get back I'll come and see you, or you might be interested in a trip to the coast. I've got to last on this ship until then. I'm sorry about your father, and I hope that he is well. It was such a

185

relief to be offered the job. I wasn't going to have to fight my way down the Nile after all. Perhaps when we're rich and famous we can cruise round the world, and I'll know people in the ports where we might call. I might be able to introduce you to some fat ex-Emperor of somewhere who runs an opium den in Macao, or we might meet some stranded Lord Jim. This is the East, you know, and such things do happen.

I think a great deal about home and about my people, and about the way things were with them. I feel such pain about leaving that place. Who would have thought it? I never thought I would miss that land. Now I'm afraid that I might forget it all. Drama, more drama! I'm homesick. I even miss seeing the old man brothel-keeper who lives next door to us. Sometimes names escape me, even after such a short time. I try to recall the streets and the colours of the houses. I'm in exile, I tell myself. It makes it easier to bear this feeling because I can give it a name that does not shame me.

Is this turning out to be too long a letter? I hope it is not too dreary. Maybe I should take up poetry. If it has any use – poetry, I mean – it can only be to make us feel that our squalid little fears and perceptions are part of a more meaningful scheme of things. I fail in this too, and I think it is a failure in generosity, a perverse need always to find fault, to look for failure and hunt it out with a kind of hard-nosed cruelty that masquerades as something noble. I spend my time in a state of shocked amazement at the way I have spent my brief life, all that endless malice, that incapacity to be warm. I spent so many years gathering resentments to myself, nurturing them on a brew that I manufactured out of the wrong done to me. Just living in that place made me feel guilty, unwanted, but as if the fault lay with me. It was that feeling of being found fault with that made me withdraw into silence.

I don't know how much of what I'm saying is making sense to you. I'm not even sure that I want to tell you all this yet. It's here now and I'm not going to change it. Perhaps it's something to do with the sea. It is so indescribably desolate and hostile. When the sea is rough, our little craft bobs on billions of cubic miles of creation as if it were not even a fragment of existence. At other times the sea is so calm, so beautifully bright and glistening, so solid-seeming, and treacherous. I hanker for the feel of good, solid earth under my feet.

I dream about you. I think about you endlessly. I never knew it would be like this, so good and yet so painful. Tell me how I'm never out of your thoughts for long. I can't wait to get back to you.

Much love,
Hassan

Also available by Abdulrazak Gurnah

Afterlives

SHORTLISTED FOR THE ORWELL PRIZE FOR
POLITICAL FICTION 2021
LONGLISTED FOR THE WALTER SCOTT PRIZE 2021

Years ago, Ilyas was stolen from his parents by the German
colonial troops. Now he returns to his village to find his parents
gone, and his sister Afiya given away. Hamza returns at the same
time. He has grown up at the right hand of an officer whose
protection has marked him for life. He seeks only work and
security – and the love of the beautiful Afiya.

As fate knots these young people together, the shadow of a
new war on another continent lengthens and darkens, ready to
snatch them up and carry them away...

'Riveting and heartbreaking ... A compelling novel, one that
gathers close all those who were meant to be forgotten, and
refuses their erasure' *Guardian*

'A brilliant and important book for our times, by a wondrous
writer' *New Statesman*, Books of the Year

'A tender account of the extraordinariness of ordinary lives ...
Exquisite' *Evening Standard*

Order your copy:
By phone: +44 (0) 1256 302 699
By email: direct@macmillan.co.uk
Delivery is usually 3–5 working days.
Free postage and packaging for orders over £20.
Online: www.bloomsbury.com/bookshop
Prices and availability subject to change without notice.
bloomsbury.com/uk/author/abdulrazak-gurnah

Gravel Heart

For seven-year-old Salim, the pillars upholding his small universe – his indifferent father, his adored uncle, his treasured books, the daily routines of government school and Koran lessons – seem unshakeable. But it is the 1970s, and the winds of change are blowing through Zanzibar: suddenly Salim's father is gone, and the island convulses with violence and corruption in the wake of a revolution.

It will only be years later, making his way through an alien and hostile London, that Salim will begin to understand the shame and exploitation festering at the heart of his family's history.

'The elegance and control of Gurnah's writing, and his understanding of how quietly and slowly and repeatedly a heart can break, make this a deeply rewarding novel' Kamila Shamsie, *Guardian*

'Riveting … The measured elegance of Gurnah's prose renders his protagonist in a manner almost uncannily real' *New York Times*

'A colourful tale of life in a Zanzibar village, where passions and politics reshape a family… Powerful' *Mail on Sunday*

Order your copy:
By phone: +44 (0) 1256 302 699
By email: direct@macmillan.co.uk
Delivery is usually 3–5 working days.
Free postage and packaging for orders over £20.
Online: www.bloomsbury.com/bookshop
Prices and availability subject to change without notice.
bloomsbury.com/uk/author/abdulrazak-gurnah

The Last Gift

Abbas has never told anyone about his past; about what happened before he was a sailor on the high seas, before he met his wife Maryam outside a Boots in Exeter, before they settled into a quiet life in Norwich with their children, Jamal and Hanna. Now, at the age of sixty-three, he suffers a collapse that renders him bedbound and unable to speak about things he thought he would one day have to.

Abbas's illness forces both children home, to the dark silences of their father and the fretful capability of their mother Maryam, who began life as a foundling and has never thought to find herself, until now.

'Gurnah writes with wonderful insight about family relationships and he folds in the layers of history with elegance and warmth' *The Times*

'A story replete with black humour and contemplative politics, told with great generosity' *Times Literary Supplement*

'At a time of forbidding public rhetoric about immigration, Gurnah's sensitive and sympathetic portrayal of his cast feels welcome' *Sunday Times*

Order your copy:
By phone: +44 (0) 1256 302 699
By email: direct@macmillan.co.uk
Delivery is usually 3–5 working days.
Free postage and packaging for orders over £20.
Online: www.bloomsbury.com/bookshop
Prices and availability subject to change without notice.
bloomsbury.com/uk/author/abdulrazak-gurnah

Desertion

SHORTLISTED FOR THE COMMONWEALTH
WRITERS' PRIZE

Early one morning in 1899, in a small town along the coast
from Mombasa, Hassanali sets out for the mosque. But he
never gets there, for out of the desert stumbles an ashen
and exhausted Englishman who collapses at his feet. That
man is Martin Pearce – writer, traveller and something of an
Orientalist. After Pearce has recuperated, he visits Hassanali to
thank him for his rescue and meets Hassanali's sister Rehana; he
is immediately captivated.

In this crumbling town on the edge of civilised life, with the
empire on the brink of a new century, a passionate love affair
begins that brings two cultures together and which will rever-
berate through three generations and across continents.

'A careful and heartfelt exploration of the way memory inevit-
ably consoles and disappoints us' *Sunday Times*

'Beautifully written and pleasurable ... The work of a maestro'
Guardian

'An absorbing novel about abandonment and loss' *Daily
Telegraph*

Order your copy:
By phone: +44 (0) 1256 302 699
By email: direct@macmillan.co.uk
Delivery is usually 3–5 working days.
Free postage and packaging for orders over £20.
Online: www.bloomsbury.com/bookshop
Prices and availability subject to change without notice.
bloomsbury.com/uk/author/abdulrazak-gurnah

By the Sea

LONGLISTED FOR THE BOOKER PRIZE 2002
SHORTLISTED FOR THE *LOS ANGELES TIMES*
BOOK AWARD

On a late November afternoon, Saleh Omar arrives at Gatwick
Airport from Zanzibar, a faraway island in the Indian Ocean.
With him he has a small bag in which lies his most precious
possession – a mahogany box containing incense. He used
to own a furniture shop, have a house and be a husband and
father. Now he is an asylum seeker from paradise; silence his
only protection.

Meanwhile Latif Mahmud, someone intimately connected with
Saleh's past, lives quietly alone in his London flat. When Saleh
and Latif meet in an English seaside town, a story is unravelled.
It is a story of love and betrayal, seduction and possession,
and of a people desperately trying to find stability amidst the
maelstrom of their times.

'One scarcely dares breathe while reading it for fear of breaking
the enchantment' *The Times*

'An epic unravelling of delicately intertwined stories, lush
strands of finely wrought narratives that criss-cross the globe ...
Astonishing and superb' *Observer*

Order your copy:
By phone: +44 (0) 1256 302 699
By email: direct@macmillan.co.uk
Delivery is usually 3–5 working days.
Free postage and packaging for orders over £20.
Online: www.bloomsbury.com/bookshop
Prices and availability subject to change without notice.
bloomsbury.com/uk/author/abdulrazak-gurnah

Admiring Silence

He thinks, as he escapes from Zanzibar, that he will probably never return, and yet the dream of studying in England matters above that. Things do not happen quite as he imagined: the school where he teaches is cramped and violent, he forgets how it feels to belong. But there is the beautiful, rebellious Emma, who turns away from her white, middle-class roots to offer him love and bear him a child. And in return he spins stories of his home and keeps her a secret from his family.

Twenty years later, when the barriers at last come down in Zanzibar, he is compelled to go back. What he discovers there, in a story potent with truth, will change the entire vision of his life.

'There is a wonderful sardonic eloquence to this unnamed narrator's voice' *Financial Times*

'I don't think I've ever read a novel that is so convincingly and hauntingly sad about the loss of home' *Independent on Sunday*

'Twisting, many-layered ... Explores themes of race and betrayal with bitterly satirical insight' *Sunday Times*

Order your copy:
By phone: +44 (0) 1256 302 699
By email: direct@macmillan.co.uk
Delivery is usually 3–5 working days.
Free postage and packaging for orders over £20.
Online: www.bloomsbury.com/bookshop
Prices and availability subject to change without notice.
bloomsbury.com/uk/author/abdulrazak-gurnah

Paradise

SHORTLISTED FOR THE BOOKER PRIZE 1994
SHORTLISTED FOR THE WHITBREAD AWARD

Born in East Africa, Yusuf has few qualms about the journey he is to make. It never occurs to him to ask why he is accompanying Uncle Aziz or why the trip has been organised so suddenly, and he does not think to ask when he will be returning. But the truth is that his 'uncle' is a rich and powerful merchant and Yusuf has been pawned to him to pay his father's debts.

Paradise is a rich tapestry of myth, dreams and Biblical and Koranic tradition, the story of a young boy's coming of age against the backdrop of an Africa increasingly corrupted by colonialism and violence.

'A poetic and vividly conjured book about Africa and the brooding power of the unknown' *Independent on Sunday*

'Lingering and exquisite' *Guardian*

'An obliterated world is enthrallingly retrieved' *Sunday Times*

Order your copy:
By phone: +44 (0) 1256 302 699
By email: direct@macmillan.co.uk
Delivery is usually 3–5 working days.
Free postage and packaging for orders over £20.
Online: www.bloomsbury.com/bookshop
Prices and availability subject to change without notice.
bloomsbury.com/uk/author/abdulrazak-gurnah

Dottie

Dottie Badoura Fatma Balfour finds solace amidst the squalor of her childhood by spinning warm tales of affection about her beautiful names. But she knows nothing of their origins, and little of her family history – or the abuse her ancestors suffered as they made their home in Britain.

At seventeen, she takes on the burden of responsibility for her brother and sister and is obsessed with keeping the family together. However, as Sophie drifts away and the confused Hudson is absorbed into the world of crime, Dottie is forced to consider her own needs. Building on her fragmented, tantalising memories, she begins to clear a path through life, gradually gathering the confidence to take risks, to forge friendships and to challenge the labels that have been forced upon her.

'Gurnah is a master storyteller' Aminatta Forna, *Financial Times*

'Astonishing, superb' *Observer*

Order your copy:
By phone: +44 (0) 1256 302 699
By email: direct@macmillan.co.uk
Delivery is usually 3–5 working days.
Free postage and packaging for orders over £20.
Online: www.bloomsbury.com/bookshop
Prices and availability subject to change without notice.
bloomsbury.com/uk/author/abdulrazak-gurnah

Pilgrims Way

Demoralised by small persecutions and the poverty of his life, Daud takes refuge in his imagination. He composes wry, sardonic letters hectoring friends and enemies, and invents a lurid colonial past for every old man he encounters. His greatest solace is cricket and the symbolic defeat of the empire at the hands of the mighty West Indies. Although subject to attacks of bitterness and remorse, his captivating sense of humour never deserts him as he struggles to come to terms with the horror of his past and the meaning of his pilgrimage to England.

'Gurnah etches with biting incisiveness the experiences of immigrants exposed to contempt, hostility or patronizing indifference on their arrival in Britain' *Spectator*

'A vibrant and vivid novel which shows human beings in all their generosity and greed, pettiness and nobility' *Herald*

'An intricate, delicate novel, vitally necessary' *New Internationalist*

Order your copy:
By phone: +44 (0) 1256 302 699
By email: direct@macmillan.co.uk
Delivery is usually 3–5 working days.
Free postage and packaging for orders over £20.
Online: www.bloomsbury.com/bookshop
Prices and availability subject to change without notice.
bloomsbury.com/uk/author/abdulrazak-gurnah